STEVIE'S PREDICAMENT

I called my friends and told them I'd hurt my bottom and I couldn't sit down.

"You mean you can't *ride*?!!" Carole said. Of course, she got it right away. So did Lisa.

"Oh, no, how are you going to get into a saddle?" Lisa asked.

I explained that I couldn't. We talked about how awful that was for a long time. See, it's very awful, so there was a lot to talk about.

The next day, we met at Pine Hollow.

By the time I reached the stable, I was crying all over again. Carole and Lisa immediately hugged me and they took me into the grain storage room.

"It just isn't fair that one of us can't ride," said Lisa.

"Right," said Carole.

I was still crying when Lisa turned to me. "I promise, Stevie, that as long as you can't ride, I won't ride."

"Me, too," said Carole.

I could hardly believe how nice my friends were being. When I think back on it, it was the craziest thing any of us had ever done, but at the time, it seemed totally logical. . . .

THE SADDLE CLUB

A SUMMER
WITHOUT HORSES

BONNIE BRYANT

A SKYLARK BOOK
NEW YORK · TORONTO · LONDON · SYDNEY · AUCKLAND

RL 5, 009-012

A SUMMER WITHOUT HORSES
A Bantam Skylark Book / July 1994

ISBN 0-553-48149-5

Published simultaneously in the United States and Canada

PRINTED IN THE UNITED STATES OF AMERICA

OPM   0   9   8

CONTENTS

PART I   Lisa's Summer   1

PART II   Stevie's Summer   63

PART III Carole's Summer   121

PART IV   Reunion   175

PART I

Lisa's Summer

IT ALL STARTED when one of my two best friends, Stevie Lake, fell out of a tree. *Slid* down is probably a more accurate way to put it. She was straddling a branch and slid down it, backside first. Unfortunately for Stevie, her three brothers were there at the time and they thought the scene was hilarious.

But Stevie wasn't exactly laughing when she ended up on the ground, fifteen feet below where she'd started from. She had an excruciating pain where she sat down (except she couldn't sit down because the pain was too excruciating).

The doctors said she had bruised her coccyx. For some people, that's not a tragedy. It just means you can't sit down for a while. But for Stevie, it was the worst possible news—if you can't sit, you can't ride a horse. And she, along with me and our other best friend, Carole Hanson, are the three most horse-crazy people I know. In fact that's why we formed The Saddle Club. It's our club and there are only two rules: Members have to be horse-crazy and they have to be willing to help one another out whenever it's necessary. It seems as if it's often necessary, especially this summer, but I'm getting to that.

Stevie can be more than a little dramatic. She told us that when the doctor said she couldn't ride for at least three weeks, her life had ended. Then, she relented a little and told us that her summer was over. I opened my mouth and said it really wasn't all *that* bad. That was the wrong thing to say because Stevie immediately turned to me and said if I didn't think it was so bad, I should try it, too. That shut me up in a hurry.

Carole was the one who suggested it first. When Stevie showed up at Pine Hollow one day crying about not being able to ride, we both felt so bad that Carole said maybe none of us should ride until Stevie could. It was a nice offer, and I'm sure Carole expected Stevie to say it wasn't necessary, but instead the opposite happened. After Carole said it, Stevie turned to her. Her eyes were round with disbelief. "You mean, you guys would actually do that for me? You and Lisa would really give up riding for three weeks? I can't believe you two. I always knew you were great friends, but this . . ." She came over to give each of us a hug.

It was a good thing Stevie hugged me just then. It was

the only way to cover up my horrified expression. At first I wanted to kill Carole, but by now Stevie was so grateful that I started to get the feeling it was the right thing to do. After all, The Saddle Club was supposed to stick together in times of trouble, and this certainly qualified.

And, after a while, I sort of got into our pact. It's like a challenging homework assignment, I told myself. And I decided to come up with a way to seal the promise.

I suggested to Stevie and Carole that if we really meant what we'd said about sticking together and not riding for three weeks, we had to find some sort of dreadful consequence. Stevie really liked that idea.

"What's the worst thing you can think of happening?" Stevie asked me eagerly.

I don't know why I said it. It just popped into my head: "Inviting Veronica diAngelo to join The Saddle Club."

Carole and Stevie both looked at me in awe, as if I'd just said the most important thing in the world.

"That's it," Stevie said.

"Absolutely the worst," said Carole.

And that was the deal. We each swore on our honor that if one of us—any one of us—rode a horse during the next three weeks, we'd have to invite the snobbiest, wormiest, laziest, vainest girl in the whole county to join our club.

Veronica diAngelo is the kind of person who believes, really *believes*, that the rest of the world was invented for her convenience and comfort. The three of us can't stand her, and just the thought of her joining our club was horrifying. It was everything we needed to stick to our guns.

The very next day, everything started to change for me. It was summer, of course, and there was no school, so I was going to Pine Hollow. That's the stable where we ride. Just because we couldn't ride didn't mean we weren't going to spend time around horses. There's always a lot to do at a stable and Max Regnery and his mother who own the place like to have everybody pitch in. They are always saying it's to keep their costs down, but the fact is that riding a horse is only a very small part of what horsemanship is about. The majority of the time with horses is spent taking care of them, grooming them, feeding them, watching them for symptoms of illness, and picking up after them. Riding was a lot of fun and the other things are a lot of work, but because they have to do with horses, they are fun work.

I was on my way out of the house when my mother walked into the kitchen. In her hands she had a lot of paper with scribbled notes. She told me she wanted to talk to me.

"It's your aunt Alison," she began. "She's been very sick, you know, and she's not getting any better."

I knew. Alison is my mother's aunt on her mother's side. I had met her once when I was about eight, and I remembered thinking she was a really nice person. Now she was sick and it didn't sound good.

Mom told me that Aunt Alison was in a nursing home in California, near Los Angeles. Mom had decided to go visit her. She didn't say "one last time," but I knew that was what she meant.

"Los Angeles?" I said, thinking quickly about all the summer days in front of me without riding. The truth is, I wouldn't have been nearly as interested in my mom's trip if I'd been planning to ride for the next three weeks. "Can I come with you?"

"I was hoping you would," Mom replied.

"Can I visit Skye Ransom, too?" I asked.

Mom smiled. "I had a feeling that would be your next question. Sure—if you can reach him."

I'm sure you've heard of Skye Ransom. Everybody has. I have a friend at school who has eight Skye Ransom posters on her ceiling—one for every movie he's starred in. I don't have any Skye Ransom posters because Skye is a friend of mine—actually of the whole Saddle Club—and I even get to see him sometimes. We met Skye while we were at a horse show in Manhattan and once he even came to Pine Hollow, to shoot a movie. It had been one of the most exciting things that had ever happened.

When I got to Pine Hollow and told Stevie and Carole about the trip, they were so excited for me they nearly burst. They are too good friends to be jealous so all they asked was that I give Skye about a million messages when I saw him. Most of Carole's messages had to do with tips about riding. Stevie's were more about how much we missed him and wished he'd do another movie in Virginia. I promised I'd tell him everything for them, especially the parts they hadn't said about how they wished they could be there with us.

"But we *will* be," Stevie said. "That's the thing about The Saddle Club. No matter where we are, we're never far apart from one another."

It sounds corny now that I'm telling you about it, but the fact is, it's true.

I LOVED CALIFORNIA from the moment we arrived. It was sunny and beautiful. Everybody there took the time to tell me that it never rains in the summer. There were palm trees and wide streets. None of the buildings I saw were very tall, though later I did see some skyscrapers in the downtown area.

Washington, the city nearest where we live, has a sort of old-fashioned elegance and style. New York, where I went with Stevie and Carole the first time we met Skye, is tall, cramped, and rushed. It always feels exciting. Los Angeles is modern, low, open, and seems much more relaxed.

In New York and Washington, the traffic jams are on the streets. In Los Angeles, they're on the freeways. As we sat in traffic on the way to our hotel, I was thinking about this and also about how much fun it was to be here, near Hollywood and where Skye lived and worked.

I still had my fingers crossed that I'd get to see Skye.

I hadn't been able to reach him before we left, although I certainly tried. First, I called his home. There was no answer and I couldn't tell how long it would be until somebody was home. Then I'd called his agent from home. It took me three tries to get past the first secretary and one more to get past the second. I bet they get a lot of calls for Skye from young girls who insist that they are Skye's friend and just want to know where they can reach him, but I think it would have been easier to get the President of the United States on the phone than Skye Ransom's agent. Finally, two days later, I got a message back from the first secretary that Skye wanted to have dinner with me the first night we were arriving in Los Angeles and would call our hotel the afternoon I arrived.

As soon as we got to the front desk at our hotel and said who we were, the man at the desk beamed at me. This was quite a change from the sullen look he'd had on his face before we told him who we were.

"You had a phone call, Ms. Atwood," he said. Then, as if it were a crown jewel, he handed me the message.

I'll pick you up at 7:30. Skye.

"Mr. Ransom called about an hour ago," the man added, as if I couldn't tell by looking at the note on the phone message. I think it was his way of telling me he knew what an important person I must be to get a phone message from a star like Skye Ransom. I hate it when people make a big deal of Skye's fame. That's not what I like about him. What I like about him is that he's a friend. Stevie probably would have known just what to say to the man who was, by then, practically bowing and drooling all over us. All I could think of was "Thank you."

A bellboy showed us to our room. It took us fifteen minutes to unpack (compared to the three hours it had taken Mom to pack) and a half hour later, we were walking up the stairs of the nursing home. It was part of an enormous hospital, but it had its own building and it didn't feel much like a hospital. I liked that. I bet the patients liked it, too.

Mom asked directions and we followed a lady along a hallway, past a lot of doors to the last room on the hall.

"Alison? Are you awake? You've got company . . ."

We went in.

The look on Aunt Alison's face when she saw my mother made me ashamed that I'd ever thought our trip out here was for anything but to see her.

"Eleanor?" she whispered.

Mom just nodded. She couldn't talk. I knew it. She was so happy to see Aunt Alison, and so upset by how sick she looked that the words just couldn't come.

"And this is Lisa?"

I nodded. I was feeling the same way as my mother was. Aunt Alison reached out her arms from her bed. We

11

both ran over and hugged her very gently. Then Aunt Alison started crying. Mom hadn't told her we were coming so she was surprised, as well as just plain happy.

It took a few minutes for everybody to get over their tears. A nurse came in with an extra chair so both Mom and I could sit down for a good long visit.

At first, Mom and Aunt Alison just caught up on things. Mom had to tell Aunt Alison about how Dad's work was going, then about her own job, then about her brother and his family and, it seemed, almost everybody else in the world. I thought it was pretty boring, but Aunt Alison seemed hungry for news and listened to everything. Then, Aunt Alison turned to me.

"Are you still horse-crazy?" she asked.

I hadn't known she'd known this about me—even if it was the most important fact. Mom must have told her sometime before, and Alison remembered.

"Absolutely," I told her. "Totally horse-crazy."

"I was, too," she said. "I think I still am, in a way."

"You ride?" The minute the words were out, I was embarrassed. She certainly wasn't riding now and hadn't been for a while. She was much too ill for that.

But Aunt Alison didn't seem bothered in the least. "You bet I do," she said. "See, even now I can't say I *did* that or I *used to*. If I could get up out of this bed today, I'd head straight for the high mountains of Montana and be in the saddle in less time than it would take you to tack up one of your fancy-bred English horses. I think that when you're really horse-crazy, you never get over it. Don't believe people who tell you that you'll outgrow it. You won't. Horses stay in the bloodstream forever."

I could have sworn she glanced at my mother when she said the part about "people who tell you." It was a sure sign to me that Mom had been telling her about my riding. Mom was a big believer in "outgrowing" horses. She didn't understand what I loved so much about horses and everything else at Pine Hollow. Obviously, Aunt Alison did.

"Did your mother ever tell you about the Montana ranch that your grandmother and I were raised on?"

"Not really," I said. "My grandmother once told me that Great-grandfather bought the land for a tune, sold it for a song, and now it's worth a whole symphony."

"If you like malls," said Aunt Alison glumly. "But it wasn't a mall then. It was beautiful green acres. Lida and I would get up before dawn sometimes and ride bareback to the hillside, where we could watch the sun come up. Then we'd race its beams back down into the valley." A sweet smile came over her face with the memory. I knew why, too. I'd done the same thing with my friends when we went out West to a dude ranch. It was such a beautiful time of day, and riding a horse that way made you feel so free. The memory made me smile as well.

"Did you get dew from the tall grass on the bottom of your bare feet?" I asked.

"Yes, child, I did. It was cool and fresh. A daily gift

13

from heaven to the beautiful meadow. My horse's belly would sometimes get wet, too, so when I groomed him, the drops would come off into his brush. I could dry my feet, but I couldn't dry his belly and Mama would always know when Lida and I had been out by our horses' legs and bellies."

I grinned. "The horses at Pine Hollow tell *our* secrets like that," I told her. "We're always supposed to walk them before we get back to the stable, but sometimes we're in a hurry and we try to get away with walking them just a little. Max, our instructor, always knows just by looking at them. That's what Stevie, one of my best friends, says. Carole—she's my other best friend—says Max knows because the horses are still lathered. Personally, I think he knows from looking at our faces. When we're guilty, we look it!"

Aunt Alison laughed. Her laugh was even nicer than her smile. "So your horse is a tattler, too. Well, sometimes they tell, but more often, they keep our secrets. I used to ride a quarter horse mare by the name of Cass. I'd go out on Cass, and Lida on her gelding. . . . I forget his name—"

"Orion," my mother said. I was astonished. I'd never known until now that my grandmother was a rider, and it made me wonder why my mother had never mentioned it before.

"Yes, Orion," Aunt Alison continued. "Cass and Orion never told about the time we went into the cave on the mountainside. Papa would have been furious if he'd ever known. He swore to us the place was filled with snakes and bats and anyone would be attacked if they went in. Naturally, we just had to go in to see if he was right."

"And? What did you find?" I asked.

"Snakes and bats," Aunt Alison said. "He was absolutely right. The first noise we made roused about a thousand bats and they all started flying around like crazy. We ran out of the place almost faster than they flew and we were on our horses and down the mountain before our fear could even catch up with us."

"What about the snakes?" I asked.

"We didn't wait around to check those out. Papa had been right about the bats. Didn't see any reason to question his judgment on the snakes."

Aunt Alison was laughing and so was I. Then we both looked at Mom. She was laughing, too.

"Mother told me that story," Mom said. "Only she told it a little differently."

"I've heard her version," said Aunt Alison. "It has me going into the cave and running out, terrified, without a bat in sight and her laughing at me. Well, don't you believe it. She was there with me and she was just as scared as I was."

My grandmother had died a long time ago so she couldn't stick up for herself. It didn't matter. The story, no matter which way was accurate, was a good one.

"I wonder about the snakes," I said.

15

"We'll never know," said Aunt Alison. "Unless, of course, I go back to the cave and look there myself, though I think it's the parking lot for a mall now. Still, I'd like to see it. In fact, if I could have just one wish, it would be to see Montana again, the beautiful land of my childhood."

I looked at the woman lying in the bed. There was a hint of the child who had been in that body once, the girlish grin and sparkle in her eyes. But now she was an old woman, weak from fighting her disease. There was no way that she'd get to Montana, short of a miracle, and that made me even sadder than knowing that she wasn't going to live very much longer.

Aunt Alison's eyes closed then and very soon she was sleeping quietly. Our visit was over.

It had been wonderful for me and I felt certain that it had been for her, too. I was very glad I'd come with Mom. Now it was time to leave. I glanced at my watch. It was time to get ready for my dinner with Skye Ransom.

No matter how far I stretched my legs in the limousine, my feet couldn't touch the back of the driver's seat. It was a very big limousine. I didn't think Skye would notice me trying, but he did.

"I can't reach, either," he said, smiling.

Skye is old enough to drive and he has his driver's license, but his parents don't like him to use their car. And the studio prefers that he use a limousine and let a professional do the driving. Skye started to explain the reason to me, but I understood it. He's a very important star to them and they don't like the idea of him driving with an inexperienced driver—himself. Life is weird when you're famous.

Most of the time when I'm with Skye I don't think about how he's famous; I think about how he's a friend.

He's just a really nice, very normal guy. He's about fifteen times better looking than any "normal" guy I know and an awful lot wealthier, but that isn't what comes through when he's with The Saddle Club.

Because he's a good friend, I can usually tell when something is bothering him and something was definitely on his mind when he picked me up. So, I asked.

"It's the picture I'm working on," he said. "Actually, it's my co-star, Chris Oliver."

I felt my heart jump. I hadn't known Skye was working with Chris Oliver! Chris Oliver was the star of a weekly television show about a group of high school students and just about every female in America between the ages of birth and twenty-five was in love with him—that is every female who wasn't already madly in love with Skye. Stevie, particularly, had a wild crush on Chris Oliver. There was an interview with him in a teen magazine that she'd read so many times the paper had started to crumble. The first thought that entered my mind after Skye mentioned him was to call Stevie and Carole—right then and there on the car phone.

Instead I tried to listen to Skye. All I said was, "Stevie was reading about him in *TeenMag*. He sounds like such a nice guy."

"He always does," Skye said. "*Sound* like a nice guy, I mean. He's spent almost every day on the set getting the director's ear to let him know what a wonderful person he is—always at my expense. If something goes wrong with a scene, Chris makes it sound like it's my fault. If something goes right, he did it. He always manages to make me look bad, or at the very least like I can't act."

"He sounds like a jerk!" I said. "What can you do about it, though?"

"Nothing." Skye sighed.

"The director has to know what's going on."

"Maybe, but maybe he doesn't. No matter what, Chris keeps going on and on with this all over the set and even in the press. He never comes out and says I'm no good or a troublemaker, he just hints and that's even worse. I've been trying to find a way to get back at him and I never seem to have an opportunity." Skye grinned at me. "What I really need is to be in another Saddle Club project, like the time you girls saved me by teaching me how to ride."

"Too bad Carole and Stevie are three thousand miles away," I reminded him.

"Well, a third of the Saddle Club is better than none of it," Skye said. Then he took my hand and squeezed it. It wasn't a boyfriend-type squeeze, it was a friend-type squeeze and it was very nice.

It seemed to me that the best thing I could do for Skye right then was to change the subject. I would have liked to talk about something cheery, but what was on my mind was Aunt Alison. I told him about visiting her in the nursing home.

"I know that place," Skye said. "It's part of the large hospital, isn't it?"

"Yes, and they're really nice in there. It's a nursing home, but you feel the 'home' part more than the 'nursing' part. They're taking really good care of Aunt Alison."

"I'm glad for that," said Skye. "The whole hospital is like that, too. In fact, I've done some work for them."

"You're a doctor?"

Skye smiled at me. "No, not like that. More like fundraising. They've got a children's wing for chronically ill kids and a wonderful research facility where they're doing ground-breaking work on some awful diseases. A friend of mine from school was a patient there and I saw all the good they were doing. I go to the wards once a week and talk with the kids there—you know, autographs, things like that. I've gotten to know some of the long-term patients pretty well. I want to make arrangements to have some of them—the ones who can—come visit a movie set I'm on sometime. Then, next week, they're having a fund-raising auction and the director of this movie I'm in has agreed to let me offer a walk-on part to the highest bidder. I'll be there to do the auction, too. That should be fun."

"You mean you're doing all those things and your director knows about them and you still think he believes it when Chris Oliver says you're a troublemaker?" I asked.

Skye was quiet for a second or two while he thought

about what I'd said. "You're amazing," he said finally. "It never occurred to me."

"Actions speak louder than words," I reminded him. "It's just that sometimes you've got to put the actions into words. I don't think you have anything to worry about. I bet he's already figured out what a creep Chris Oliver is."

I couldn't believe I was using the words "creep" and "Chris Oliver" in the same sentence, and maybe Stevie would never forgive me, but we were loyal friends to Skye and if Skye said Chris Oliver was a creep, it had to be true. I decided that I'd explain it all to Stevie when I got home.

"I'm glad you're here," Skye said, squeezing my hand again.

"Me, too, but speaking of 'here,' where are we?"

"We're almost at the restaurant," he said. "We're going to Penelope's."

"*Penelope's!*" I knew from reading tons of magazines that Penelope's is *the* hangout for stars and Hollywood glitterati. It's the kind of place where autograph hounds and photographers just stand around, waiting for famous people to show up. And *I* was going there with *Skye Ransom!* Two thoughts flashed through my head as the limousine pulled up to the curb: First, I wished I'd worn something newer and a little more trendy; second, I wished Stevie and Carole were with me.

The limousine drew to a stop. The driver got out and stepped around to open the door. It was the door on my side so I got out first. I could see people peering in to see who would emerge. When they saw it was me, their faces fell and they lowered their cameras. But when I was followed by Skye, I could hear the "ooohs" and "aaahs." Cameras started flashing and a couple of girls reached out to touch him. Three pads and pens appeared. Skye signed them and then shook hands with the swooning girls. He gave everyone a smile, a nice, genuine, Skye Ransom smile, and we began the walk into Penelope's. Just as we did that, another car pulled up and out stepped Chris Oliver!

4

THERE WAS ANOTHER round of "oohs" and "aaahs"; the hands reached out, the autograph pads appeared. Chris Oliver ignored them all, brushing the hands and pads aside, smiling only for the cameras. That was when I really understood what Skye had been telling me. Chris Oliver was a phony. All he cared about was publicity, not the fans who had made him the star he was.

Chris was followed out of the car by a breathtakingly beautiful young girl. Chris was about twenty-two, if Stevie's magazine was right. This girl had to be about eighteen. She was wearing a dress that dipped and curved in places I didn't think I'd ever have and if I did, my parents wouldn't let me wear the dress to show them off until I was well into my forties!

"Skye! Oh, Skye, my good man!" Chris called out

heartily. *My good man?* I don't think I've ever heard anyone under about sixty use that phrase. "What a nice surprise to see you here. Why don't we join up and dine
together!"

That was about the last thing in the world Skye wanted
to do. And in spite of the fact that it would be very cool
to have dinner with not one but two of Hollywood's biggest hunks, I just wanted to be with Skye. Still, what
could we do? Skye was too polite to turn down the invita-
tion, and besides, even a Hollywood newcomer like me
knew this was good publicity for their movie.

"Sure," Skye mumbled, and the next thing I knew, I
was seated in a booth with the two of them and Chris's
date, who was introduced to me as Krysti. She spelled it
for me, just to be sure I had it. Then she explained that it
was the only name she had. "Like Cher," she said. I tried
not to roll my eyes. Krysti was what Stevie would have
called an airhead. I just ignored her. It wasn't hard to do.

Skye introduced me to Chris and Krysti ("Don't you
love how our names are practically the same?" she
squealed) as his riding instructor. That confused both of
them, but it was all right. It gave me a certain status and
that was good. Then a couple of photographers came and
snapped pictures of the four of us. I could imagine myself
on the covers of newspapers at supermarkets all over the
world. I asked Skye if that might happen.

Chris answered for him. "You bet it can and you never

can tell what they'll say about you in the articles. I can see it now. 'Riding Instructor Named in Love Triangle!' "

I giggled, visualizing the reactions of my friends and family: Stevie would think it was funny; Carole would be horrified because I really didn't have enough riding experience to be called an instructor; my mother would just about die of embarrassment. This could be interesting!

The menus arrived along with a waiter only too happy for the honor of announcing the evening's specials to Skye and Chris. This was all so exciting to me that I didn't think I'd be able to eat anything. When the waiter came back for our orders, I still hadn't made up my mind.

Chris took over, as if he were the father or something. He ordered for Krysti and himself, then he looked at me. I guess he saw some confusion on my face so he started making suggestions and translating the menu—as if I didn't know that *homard* meant lobster and *veau* was veal. In a way, he was being nice, but in another way, it was a sort of a putdown, making the waiter think I was some sort of ignoramus.

"I'll have the *escargots* to start and then the *venaison* for my main course," I said. I knew perfectly well I'd just ordered snails and deer, two things I don't much like to eat, especially when I'm not hungry, but I felt this wild urge to show Chris that I knew how to read a menu, and, even more important, how to pronounce the French properly.

I didn't have much time to think about how I'd eat

what I'd ordered because that's when the reporter showed up. Both Skye and Chris knew who she was. Krysti sat up straighter when she heard her name, Nancy Lamport. Even I sort of recognized it. She's a major Hollywood reporter. Everybody reads her daily column and she can make or break a movie—or a star—with a stroke of her word processor. The fact that she'd come to our table meant that Skye's movie might get some coverage. Whether it was good or bad largely depended on what happened in the next five minutes.

"Now, don't tell me how wonderful your movie is," Ms. Lamport began, cutting off Chris before he could launch into a big speech. "I can get that from your publicity department. Tell me what you're doing that's going to make it a smash hit."

Chris wasted no time. "As you know, the movie is about two brothers who become lost in the wilderness. I think the essence of the film lies in the feelings of desolation, isolation, and loss. To convey this to the movie-going public, it must come from within. I have techniques I developed with my acting coach, Igor Novolovsky. One, for example, involves climbing into my shower stall, nude."

How else would you get into the shower? I wondered. But there was more. I listened, now truly understanding Skye's problem with this guy. Phony didn't begin to cover the subject.

"I've had the glass door painted black so I am totally

isolated. I turn on the water, to an unbearably cold temperature. I am alone, utterly alone. I feel it to my core. Then the tears come, mingling with the cold water. When I can bear it no more, I scream. The isolation is complete and when I perform for the camera, I draw on that."

Ms. Lamport was writing as fast as she could. I guess she didn't want to miss a word. I had the feeling that when it came out in print, it would have the effect of making Chris look like a very serious performer instead of the big phony he was.

When the reporter's pencil stopped, she looked at Skye. "And how do you spend your time when you're not actually on the set?" she asked. "Do you have techniques, too?"

He was still stunned by what Chris had said. "Nothing like that," Skye began, nearly stammering.

I couldn't keep quiet any longer. Skye had said he needed Saddle Club help, so he got it.

"He doesn't have to," I said. "Everyone who has ever seen Skye on a screen knows that he's a wonderful actor, don't you agree?"

Ms. Lamport agreed. At least she nodded.

"And besides, he's too busy with the other things he does."

"Sports and things like that?" she asked me.

"Some, but Skye would never let anything interfere with the work he does at the Dade Children's Hospital."

"Really?" Now she seemed interested. "Tell me about it."

Skye did. He told her everything he'd told me and she wrote it all down. When Chris tried to mention that he'd helped out at a homeless shelter once, she practically ignored him. I remembered the story, too. There had been a big celebrity "do" for a shelter in Beverly Hills—where homeless means you only rent. Nobody was impressed by Chris's big heart.

Ms. Lamport stayed at our table for quite a while, talking with Skye about the upcoming fund-raising auction at Dade and about his work with the kids there. Skye's face lit up as he told her about one little boy who had taken his first steps into Skye's arms and how much that meant to Skye.

When her notebook was full, Ms. Lamport stood up, thanked Skye and then Chris, nodded to Krysti, shook my hand, and left.

The rest of the evening was both wonderful and too ridiculous for words. Chris was in a huff and was very rude, mostly to poor Krysti. When we went to the ladies' room together, I expected her to burst into tears. Instead she seemed oblivious, and told me all about the plastic surgery she thought she'd have over the next couple of years. If I don't recognize her next time I see her, I decided, that's okay with me.

As soon as we were done eating, Chris and Krysti left. Skye and I enjoyed the rest of our evening together.

When we left Penelope's—to more flashbulbs and auto-graph pads—we got in the car, and he and the chauffeur took me on a guided tour of Los Angeles by night. We saw everything from Hollywood Boulevard (very tacky) to Mulholland Drive (breathtaking). It was great and it was over too soon except for the fact that my yawns kept informing me, as well as Skye, that my body thought it was three hours later than the car clock said it was.

Skye took me back to the hotel, gave me a hug, and put me in the elevator. Mom wanted to hear everything, but I told her she could read about it in the morning. I was in bed and asleep within minutes.

I'D BEEN JOKING, of course, when I told my mother she
could read all about it, but it turned out that it wasn't a
joke at all. I awoke to my mother's screams.

"Lisa! Lisa! You won't believe this! Lisa!" she cried,
running into the bedroom from the sitting room and waving a newspaper at me. "Look at this! You're here and so
is Skye!!!"

I sat bolt upright in bed and looked at the clock. I
barely had time to register the fact that it was 7:30 in the
morning when the phone rang.

It was closest to me so I picked it up automatically.
"Lisa Atwood, you're a miracle worker!" declared a famil-
iar voice. "I couldn't have made it all come out better if
I'd done it myself. It's the old Saddle Club magic, isn't it?
You are *some*thing!"

Through the haze of morning sleepiness, I began to recognize where I was and what was happening. I was in Los Angeles, California, in a hotel with my mother who was hysterical with joy for some reason, still flapping the newspaper in my direction. I was talking on the phone with somebody who loved me. I recognized the voice from somewhere. . . .

It came to me. It was Skye. As he went on, the words "newspaper" and "column" and "Lamport" came through strongly enough for me to think that my mother's actions and Skye's words were somehow related.

"Stop! Everybody stop!" I said. "I don't know what you're talking about."

"Nancy Lamport's column," Skye said. "She wrote up everything I said last night. Listen to this: 'While some young actors seem more concerned with bizarre techniques that make them look like the professionals that they clearly are not, others, like Skye Ransom, are busy with the business of humanity. This bright, young, handsome star, accompanied by a charming girl named Lisa Atfield'—I'm sorry she got it wrong, Lisa, but that's the way she spelled it—'was dining last night at Penelope's and took time out from a social dinner to tell this reporter about the work he's doing with chronically ill kids at Dade.'"

Skye took a breath. Mom handed me the newspaper and pointed to the column. It was a big story, two full

columns, headed by the words, SKYE RANSOM, HUMANITAR-
IAN. Skye read to me, and I read along, loving every word.

"Imagine all the good this is going to do!" Skye said.

Yes, I thought to myself. It's going to let the world
know what a terrific guy Skye is. That wasn't what Skye
had in mind, however.

"With publicity like this, hundreds, maybe even thousands, more people will come to the charity auction! The
kids! It's going to be great for them. So much money for
research . . ."

And that told me that Skye Ransom was every bit as
great a guy as I'd always thought. He'd been worried about
Chris making him look bad, and when the opportunity
arrived to make Chris look bad, all Skye really cared
about was the good that was going to come out of it for
the hospital. In case I'd ever wondered why I liked Skye
Ransom so much (which I hadn't, by the way), there was
the answer to the question.

"Lisa, there's no way I can thank you for what you did.
I was just sitting there at the table last night, trying to
think of something to say, and you came through. You got
me started talking about something that really mattered.
It matters to me and it matters to a lot of sick children. It
matters a whole lot more than Chris screaming in a black-
ened shower stall."

"You don't have to thank me," I told him. "Just knowing that Chris got put in his place *and* you're going to

have a chance to help more kids is enough thanks for me."

"Well, it's not enough for me," Skye said. "And I think I'll have a way to repay you, just a little bit. I got a call early this morning from the production supervisor. They need to work on some of Chris's solo scenes today so they don't need me at all. I've got a surprise day off. When can you be ready?

"For what?" I asked.

"To go for a ride—a *horse*back ride. I know you must miss riding with your friends while you're out here so I've arranged to have horses for us at a stable in the valley, north of the city. I can be there to pick you up in about an hour. We'll have about a one-hour drive and then all day to ride and hang out. Okay?"

"Just a sec," I said.

I had to talk to my mother, but I also had to talk to myself. First there was Aunt Alison, but I knew she'd understand about riding. Then there was The Saddle Club. If I went for a ride with Skye, I'd be breaking a vow. And—thanks to my own brilliant suggestion—if I said yes to Skye I'd have to invite Veronica diAngelo to join the club. My friends would never forgive me.

If they found out.

How could they find out? I wouldn't tell. I could ask Skye not to tell. He'd understand, for sure. He disliked Veronica almost as much as we did. Mom wouldn't tell, though sometimes I think she wants me to be Veronica's friend. Mom likes the idea of all the social power the diAngelos have in Willow Creek. Still, if I asked her nicely, she wouldn't tell anyone.

My conscience pricked me again. I had made a pledge to my best friends. Stevie couldn't ride, so Carole and I couldn't ride.

This wasn't just a ride, though, this was a chance to spend a whole day with Skye Ransom. I could see it—the two of us on our horses, riding across the craggy California mountains, or down by the Pacific Ocean, racing the waves, climbing off our horses and walking in the gentle surf. Just me and Skye, no photographers, no airhead starlets, no chauffeur, no Chris Oliver. How could I possibly say no?

"Forty-five minutes," I told Skye.

"I'll be there," he said.

THE PLACE WHERE we live, Willow Creek, Virginia, is hilly
country. Everywhere you look, there are gentle rolling
hills. Los Angeles is hilly country, too, but it's not at all
like home. In Los Angeles you can be driving along a
perfectly nice, flat, straight road, then within a matter of
seconds, find yourself on a very curvy mountain road. It's
very dramatic, but I was beginning to feel that everything
in Los Angeles was very dramatic.

We were going up what I thought was our second
mountain when Skye noticed that I was wearing jeans, a
polo shirt, and a pair of paddock boots.

"Where are your real riding clothes?" he asked.

"This is what I've got. I wasn't planning to do any
riding, so I didn't bring my boots and hard hat. I hope this
is okay."

He smiled his million-dollar smile at me. "Of course it is. You can wear whatever you want, as long as it's safe."

One of the other things I really like about Skye is that he understands what's important. Fancy riding clothes are nice, but safe riding clothes are important.

After about four hundred curves, turns, and dips on the mountain road, we were suddenly in a valley and then in some more mountains and then, with one final turn, we were there.

The Double H was a huge stable surrounded by rings and paddocks. Several riders were working on a jumping course, while others worked with cavaletti, and another was lunging her horse. I took a deep breath as I looked around. It was great to be back around horses. The only thing missing was Stevie and Carole. I felt a twinge of guilt. It bothered me so much that I spaced out for the next few minutes, until Skye introduced me to my horse for the day.

His name was Kip. He was a chestnut gelding with three white socks. He was very tall and elegant and at first I thought he was a Thoroughbred.

"Not quite," Mr. Ward, the owner of Double H, said. "He's only half Thoroughbred, but when you ride him, you'll find that it's the bigger half. He's a wonderful horse. I know you'll enjoy this ride."

I thought it was funny the way he described Kip as having a "bigger half." I knew just what he meant.

I'm not the expert that Carole and Stevie are, and I

know I've made mistakes judging horses by their looks, but one look at Kip and I knew he was a good one. I turned out to be exactly right, too.

Mr. Ward put Skye on a bay named Chesapeake. Some stables choose their horses' names in themes and a quick look around at the nameplates of the bay horses at the Double H confirmed that this was one of those stables. Their other bays were named things like Hudson, Cape Cod, Biscayne, and Botany. They were a real geography lesson in the bays of the world!

Twenty minutes later Skye and I were mounted and ready to go. Skye had just one more surprise for me and that was when the limo driver pulled a picnic for each of us out of the trunk of the car. They were packed in backpacks so we could ride with them. I knew it was going to be a perfect day.

Skye was familiar with the land around the Double H and Mr. Ward told us where to head for views and safe riding. We were off.

Skye had learned a lot about riding since the first time we'd met. He was comfortable at a walk, trot, and canter, at least on level ground, and he knew how to handle his horse well. Since I was the more experienced rider, I rode behind. The best rider should always be at the back in case something happens to someone up ahead.

The trail was incredibly dramatic. The path snaked up a hillside and every time we cut a turn, it almost took my breath away to see how high we were and how far we could see. There were vast sections of towns and villages in the valley on one side of the hill and on another, there were endless stretches of hills, cliffs, canyons, and gorges. When we rounded the mountain we were climbing, suddenly there was the Pacific, stretching to the horizon. Skye stopped Chesapeake to look and I pulled up alongside him.

"Beautiful, isn't it," I said.

"Yes," he agreed. "I feel so far away from Hollywood when I'm here. That's why I love this trail." He glanced at me. "You help me with that, too," he went on.

"Me?"

"Yes, you and Stevie and Carole," he said. "I always think of you three as my *good* friends because you're good for me. You three somehow manage to treat me as a human being and not as a superstar. Does that sound stupid?"

"No," I told him firmly. "After seeing what happens when you go out, it makes total sense to me."

Skye went on. "When the reporter wrote her column about me, all she was thinking about was the superstar part, but when you said the things you did, and started me talking about the things I do that I think are the most important and that I'm able to do for other people only because I *am* a superstar, well"—he looked at me and gave me that smile—"it was another way of being good for me. I had only been thinking about showing Chris up by being a professional superstar. You made it possible to show him up by being a human. There aren't enough ways to thank you for that, Lisa."

With those words, he reached out, took my hand, and then leaned over and kissed me.

It's true. Absolutely. I've been kissed by Skye Ransom.

When we broke apart I was shaking. I know it sounds silly, but I've only been kissed by two other boys and there's something so special about Skye, even though it was a friendly-type kiss. At that moment what I wanted, more than anything in the world, was to tell Carole and Stevie all about it. But I couldn't. I couldn't tell them about the horses and the mountain and the trail and the Pacific. I couldn't tell them any of that and I probably couldn't even tell them about the kiss because they'd want a zillion details and I couldn't give them the details without letting them know I'd been riding. I gulped, almost wishing it hadn't happened.

"Come on," Skye said, interrupting my thoughts. "The place I want to have lunch is right up ahead a little and it's got an entirely different view from this one. Just wait until you see it."

There was a sort of plateau around the bend. It looked like the kind of place a Department of Highways would call Scenic View, except that there were no cars and no other people. It was panoramic. We could see mountains, valleys, gulches, hills, canyons, cities, and sky.

I know we ate the picnic because after we'd been there for fifteen minutes, I felt full and there was no more food in our packs, but I was too enthralled with the view to notice what I was eating. Skye talked while we ate, too, and I do remember that. He talked about his movie and about Chris Oliver and how much it meant to him to have me help him with his career.

I don't want anyone to get the wrong idea about what was happening. Just because Skye Ransom kissed me and just because he was telling me how much I meant to him, he wasn't being a boyfriend. That wasn't it at all, and one of the other things I like best about Skye Ransom is that we both knew that and neither of us had to say anything about it. Skye is much older than I am. He's seventeen and I'm only thirteen. I don't think he has many friends his own age. He doesn't go to a regular school because he's always working on a movie so he has his own tutor. He spends most of his time with adults, and the kids he knows are other professionals like Chris Oliver. That's not exactly what I call a friend. To Skye, I am a friend, the same way I am with Stevie and Carole. It's almost as if we're the ones who get to teach him what being a kid is about. That's something I'm glad to do for a friend.

After lunch we rode back down to the Double H. The jump course was empty. I really wanted to try Kip out on it and Mr. Ward said it was okay. He even found a hard hat for me to use. Skye sat on the fence and watched. He's okay on a flat course, but he hasn't done much jumping yet and he didn't want to try.

Kip was a dream jumper. Carole's always reminding me

that every horse has things they are good at and things they aren't so good at. So far, Carole's formula wasn't working for Kip. It seemed to me that he was wonderful at absolutely everything. Max says that the most important thing in hunter jumping is to maintain an even pace and to leave the ground the right distance in front of the jump for the jump. Kip acted as if he'd listened to every word Max had said! Even Skye could tell that I was having a good time and was doing a good job. When I finished the jump course for the second time, I drew Kip to a walk and we ambled over to where Skye was sitting on the fence. I must have had a big grin on my face.

"Like him?" Skye asked.

"Oh, he's wonderful!" I said.

"Good. Because he's yours."

"He's what?" I asked, assuming I'd misheard Skye. I unsnapped my hard hat so I could hear better.

"Yours. He's *yours*."

"Mine?"

I couldn't believe it. What Skye was telling me was that he'd just arranged with Mr. Ward to buy the horse for me. Mr. Ward was working on hiring a plane to fly Kip back to Virginia to Pine Hollow the following week.

Mine? Skye had bought the horse for *me*? He said it was because I'd helped him with Chris Oliver. It was the most incredible moment of my life. I know I started crying, but I didn't pay any attention to the tears. There was too much else to think about. Kip wasn't just some nag. He was a really good horse and Skye was chartering a whole airplane just to have him flown to Virginia! For *me*!

Suddenly I felt like a different person. I wasn't just Lisa Atwood, rider. I was Lisa Atwood, horse owner. Better still, Lisa Atwood, Kip owner. The words began to sink in. I leaned way forward in the saddle and gave Kip the biggest hug around his neck that I could manage. It also gave me a chance to wipe my tears of happiness off in Kip's mane. I didn't want Skye to think he'd just gone to a lot of trouble to buy a wonderful horse for a baby.

For a minute, I tried to protest.

"You don't have to do that, Skye. I don't really need a horse. This is much too expensive a gift. I couldn't possibly repay you."

"Lisa," he said. "You're my friend. I can afford a generous present for a girl who's generous with her friendship. Elvis used to buy Cadillacs for strangers. The least Skye can do is to buy a horse for a friend. Please?"

What could I say, but "Thank you"? And then a minute later, "Thank you very much. More than I can tell you." Then I hugged Kip again and told him he was going to have to learn to whinny with a gentle Southern drawl because he was moving to Virginia!

"BE CAREFUL WHAT you wish for. It may come true."

I'd always thought that was a dumb proverb until it happened to me. My dream of a lifetime was about to be fulfilled and by the time I got out of Skye's limousine at the hotel, I was beginning to see the bad side of it all.

I should have seen it right away, but it's hard to be logical when a movie star gives you a horse and tells you he's going to have it flown across the country for you. When something that wonderful happens, it's hard to remember that there is any bad news anywhere in the world.

But there was bad news—and it was that Veronica di-Angelo was about to become a member of The Saddle Club.

That was the thought that filled my mind as I walked

into the hotel lobby that afternoon. In the elevator, I began manufacturing stories in my mind. What could I possibly tell Stevie and Carole so they wouldn't know I'd been riding in California? It seemed so cruel, like something out of a horror movie: Now that I finally had my own horse, I'd be stuck with Veronica diAngelo in The Saddle Club!

By the time I reached our floor I realized lying to my two best friends would feel terrible. I opened the door to our room and saw my mother sitting reading a book. Oh no, I thought. How are my parents ever going to afford what it will cost to feed and board Kip? Horses are expensive to own.

"How was your ride?" Mom asked.

"Great," I answered truthfully. "Skye is the most wonderful, generous person I've ever known."

My mother beamed. There's a part of her that's just thrilled that her daughter is friends with *the* Skye Ransom, and then there's another part of her that just plain likes Skye. Skye is one thing she and I agree on totally.

"He had a picnic made for us and we rode up into the mountains and he kept telling me how much what I'd done had meant to him and I kept telling him how it really wasn't any big deal and we just had a good time."

Of course I didn't tell her that Skye hadn't just given me a picnic lunch. He'd also given me a horse. I felt so totally confused about Kip and what he was going to mean to The Saddle Club as well as to the Atwood family

44

that I just wasn't ready to tell. I knew I had some thinking to do and Mom couldn't help me.

Since we'd both had long days and were tired, we ordered dinner in the room. I haven't stayed in hotels much, but I have to say I just love it when they wheel a table into your room and it's got all this clean white linen on it and plates covered with silver things to keep the food warm. There was even a little flower on the table. It wasn't exactly a picnic on a hillside overlooking most of southern California, but it was a nice dinner for my mother and me.

I'd ordered a steak and it smelled delicious. It was, too.

"How was Aunt Alison today?" I asked.

"She's okay."

That was all my mother said and it told me an awful lot. The fact that she gave me only two words meant that Aunt Alison really wasn't okay and Mom didn't want me to worry. That gave me one more thing to worry about.

We talked a lot, but said very little, mostly chatting about how we needed to send postcards to friends and family. I knew there was something my mother didn't want to tell me about. I wondered if she knew there was something I wasn't telling her. We finished up our dinner and were in bed early. We both wrote out a couple of postcards and then turned out the lights.

I don't think I slept at all that night. First, I'd think about lying to my friends and when that made me feel really awful, I'd think about Kip. Then I'd think about ruining The Saddle Club by having Veronica in it and when that made me feel really awful, I'd think about Kip. Then I'd think about how much it was going to cost to house, feed, and care for Kip and when that made me feel really awful, I'd think about riding Kip. And then I'd think about not having Kip and the fact that I was already planning to lie to my friends, because not telling something can be just as much of a lie as telling something and when those thoughts made me feel really awful, I'd think about Kip again.

Nobody in the world could sleep with thoughts like that tumbling around in her head. I'd gone to bed feeling miserable and confused and by the time the sun came up, I felt miserable, confused, *and* tired.

Since I hadn't decided yet what I was going to do, I decided not to think about it for the whole day. Mom had our day all planned. We were going to visit the Los Angeles County Museum in the morning, then have lunch in Beverly Hills at a nice little restaurant she'd read about, then we'd go visit Aunt Alison.

I know it sounds boring, but it really wasn't at all. I had a good time with Mom. She knows a lot about art and was able to help me see and understand things I wouldn't have otherwise seen. We spent a long time studying the Impressionist paintings, which I used to think just looked fuzzy—as if the painters needed new glasses. Mother explained to me that they were experimenting with light and color, showing what light did to and for perception. Also they were painting the things of everyday life—people, objects, places, and that was very different from the painters who came before them who tended to deal with grand or famous or historical subjects.

After that, we looked at some paintings of horses and hunting. I explained some of the finer points of horses to her. She's always thought that how a horse looks is the most important thing about it. I was finally able to convince her that looks were the least important factor. It's how well the horse performs the job he's expected to do, whether that's pulling a heavy wagon to market or jumping over a fence after a fox.

The restaurant in Beverly Hills had an outdoor garden with tables in it. I know I spent too much time looking at the people around us and wondering if any of them were rich and famous, and I was aware that my mother was doing the same thing. But there must have been some people there who wondered if Mom and I were rich and famous! Star-gazing is a two-way street.

Then we went to see Aunt Alison. Mom seemed relieved the minute we saw her and that confirmed my suspicion that Aunt Alison had been having a bad day the day before and Mom hadn't wanted to tell me just how bad it was. My great-aunt was sick, of course, but she had a warm smile on her face when we walked into her room.

"Lisa, tell me about your ride yesterday!" she said eagerly.

She wanted every single detail of every minute of it and I was only too happy to fill her in.

"Kip sounds like a wonderful horse!" she said.

"He absolutely is. I think he's the best all-round horse I've ever ridden. You should have seen how he took the jumps. I mean you should have felt it!"

"Oh, that's right. It's English riding you do, isn't it? We never did much jumping in Montana. We just rounded up cattle."

That got me talking about my Western riding—the times I've gone with Stevie and Carole to our friend Kate's dude ranch.

"I've been on some cattle drives and I've camped out. In fact, we even had a race with a forest fire!"

"Fires on a dry day can be deadly," Aunt Alison said.

"Especially when there's a breeze," I agreed. "For a while there, I wasn't sure we were going to make it."

"Now, now, Lisa," Mother said. "Don't you go making up stories for Aunt Alison."

"I'm not making it up, Mom. It happened."

"It did?"

The look on my mother's face reminded me that I might not have given her exactly all the details of our pack trip, and the look also reminded me why. My mother could be so overprotective sometimes. It was too late now and besides, what did it matter? I was home safely.

"There was a fire near our ranch one very dry summer," Aunt Alison went on. "It came across our land and killed half the herd of cattle, but it jumped over most of our garden. They do that, you know—jump, I mean."

49

"I know. It's one of the reasons they can move so fast sometimes."

"Oh, that land," she said. Once again, she sounded wistful. "It was truly God's country. I can remember thinking sometimes that land went on forever. Sometimes all I could see were the mountains, sometimes just the prairies. And everywhere there was the blue sky. It stretched on for all eternity."

"Big Sky country, right?" I asked.

"Yes," she said, sighing.

I realized that the very thought of Montana was comforting to her.

"You think about it a lot, don't you?" I asked.

"All the time," she said. "I think it's because it occupies so much of my mind and fills my heart with happiness that I don't have room in my brain to think about this disease and the pain it's causing me."

Aunt Alison shifted her position in her bed and although she didn't say anything, I could see that the movement had been painful to her. She pulled the covers up with her thin, white hands. It was a simple movement, one I make every night, but I could see that it wasn't simple for her and the whiteness of her hands reminded me that she'd been in this bed and in this hospital for a very long time. That, more than anything, made me sad, because I've always loved being outdoors—especially when being outdoors included being with horses.

I didn't say anything then. I just waited and watched. Aunt Alison wanted to say something else.

"At night, I close my eyes and pretend I'm in Montana. I know the place I grew up isn't there anymore, but a lot of the state is still just about the way I remember it: wild, mountainous, craggy, open, and beautiful. It's as if it calls to me. Sometimes I wonder what heaven is like and if I'll get there. One night I decided that I only want to go there if it's just like Montana."

"Would you like to go to Montana again?" I asked. I don't know why I asked it. It was a foolish question and the minute it was out of my mouth, I regretted it, for in that instant, Aunt Alison's eyes filled with tears.

"More than anything," she whispered. Her eyes closed then and she slept. Mother and I left her alone.

We didn't talk much on the way back to our hotel. We'd both been moved by Aunt Alison's passion and saddened by her sadness. Aunt Alison had also made me think about Pepper, the horse I'd learned to ride on, who'd gotten ill and had been put down last fall.

I don't mean to say that an animal's death is the same as a person's. What I thought about was the fact that Pepper had lived a good life. He'd done everything a stable horse could do by the time he was old and dying. If he'd known what regrets were, he wouldn't have had any. But Aunt Alison had regrets. She missed Montana and she wasn't going to be able to get on an airplane and fly back there one more time. That made me sad. It also made me think about regrets. Sometimes regrets are about things you've done; sometimes they're about things you haven't done. Sometimes they're unavoidable; sometimes they aren't.

The phone was ringing when we got back to our room. I grabbed it and heard Skye's voice.

"I'm so glad you're there, Lisa," he began. "I've got everything set for chartering the plane to take Kip back to Virginia. The charter people just want to know exactly when they should plan to arrive. Have you talked to Max yet?"

I hesitated, then said, "I can't accept Kip, Skye."

"Why not?" he asked.

I could have explained about our pledge in The Saddle Club and about Veronica diAngelo and he would have understood, but it wasn't the real reason. It was only half the reason. The other half was the expense that my parents simply couldn't afford. They'd considered buying me a horse at one time, and we'd even looked at quite a few. Since that time, they'd learned more about how much a horse costs to keep and it's a lot of money. The better the horse, the more money. Kip would be well beyond our budget and I knew it. It wasn't fair to ask my parents to do something I knew they couldn't afford.

I began to explain that to Skye.

"I want you to have this horse, Lisa. I think he's perfect for you. You said so yourself. Giving him to you is the best way I can think of to thank you for what you did for me. Can I help to convince your parents?"

"No, please," I said. "Kip is wonderful and perfect, but I just can't accept him. The wonderful day you and I had yesterday is more than enough thanks for what I did. Really."

"Oh, come on," Skye said. "There must be something —I mean, Lisa, if you don't let me do something for you, I won't feel as if I've thanked you properly."

Then it came to me. I guess I already had this image of the airplane specially designed to carry horses, just waiting at the airport for my horse. It popped into my head then that there were other airplanes that were specially designed for various purposes, including ambulances.

"Aunt Alison—" I blurted out.

"What?"

"Remember my aunt—the one in the hospital?"

"Of course. I'm going to stop and visit her next time I'm seeing the kids there."

"Well, if you're really in the mood to charter airplanes, how about an ambulance plane that can make a nice little round trip to Montana?"

9

It was a day I'll never forget.

In the first place, it took about four hundred phone calls, including one to the hospital, a private nursing service as well as Aunt Alison's doctor, and then to the ambulance services and then probably to the FAA for all I know, but it was arranged. It was scheduled for two days later, but Aunt Alison was having a bad time that day, so everything had to be put off for a day.

One of the nicest things was that we didn't tell her about the trip until the ambulance showed up to take her to the airport at seven o'clock in the morning.

"Where am I going?" she asked.

Mom looked at me. "Montana," I said. "I promise to tell you the whole story on the airplane."

Aunt Alison was speechless and that was okay because

if she'd been talking, I might have had to talk and I don't think I could have.

Mom, Aunt Alison, and I rode in the ambulance to the airport. Skye met us there. I loved the fact that he wanted to come along and it coincided with a day he had off the set. The ambulance drove right up to the airplane and Aunt Alison was put aboard in a comfortable bed. Since it was going to be a couple of hours until we got to the Big Sky country (and I was now thinking of it totally as the Big Skye country), the nurse gave Alison some medicine so she would sleep. Mom, Skye, and I went into the passenger cabin where there was a nice breakfast spread out for us.

I could almost feel it when we got to Montana. Below us, the Rockies seemed cleaner, higher, shinier, and more snow-covered. There were fewer towns and more greenery.

I went into Aunt Alison's cabin. Her eyes were opened.

"We're there, aren't we?" she asked. I knew she'd felt it, too.

It was a sparkling clear day. As the pilot descended through the sky, Aunt Alison and I looked out the window.

"We had a pasture just like that one," she said, pointing. "And we kept our horses there just like that." I looked where she pointed. There was a herd of horses. Our plane was low enough now for them to be able to hear the sound. One, a big bay, looked up at us and then rose in a magnificent rear that startled the whole herd into action. They galloped across the meadow, racing the small shadow of the plane.

"There's one there—the Appaloosa, see him? It looks just like Cass! Gallops like her, too. How she used to love to run, that horse! Oh, Lisa!" she said. I know I wasn't paying for the plane ride, but as far as I was concerned, the joy in her voice was enough payment for ten ambulance planes to Montana. She was breathless with excitement.

She reached for my hand and squeezed it. She never let go of it for the whole rest of the visit to Montana, either. She held tightly as we swooped around the mountains, bringing her closer than she'd ever been on horseback. She held my hand as we entered a valley. There was a small ranch nestled among a stand of trees at one end and it had a flourishing vegetable garden between it and the barn. The barn was surrounded by animals in pens, pigs, sheep, goats, and a larger area where some cows stood, contentedly munching on grass. Beyond their field lay the meadows where the cattle grazed. Aunt Alison gave my hand a little squeeze then. I knew it was because that ranch reminded her of her girlhood home. The plane made a turn then, heading farther north.

"Approaching ground zero," the pilot announced. Aunt Alison looked a little confused.

"You'll see," I said. "Just wait."

Aunt Alison did see. She saw everything. She sat as far

56

upright in her bed as she could manage and watched out the window for every single detail she could get of Montana. Then the wild country changed into a settled area below us. It wasn't exactly a city, but there were a lot of houses and streets and then there was a small shopping mall.

I waited quietly to see if she would recognize anything specific. Then a look came across her face as she stared at the craggy top of one of the mountains.

"It's Bison Rock! I know it. There it is!" She took a deep breath. "I'm home," she said.

"What's Bison Rock?"

"Well, just look," she said. "See how the rock there on the side of the mountain is shaped sort of like the back and head of a buffalo?"

I looked. I couldn't see it at all, but I had a feeling that it was clearer when you were on horseback than in an airplane. The important thing was that Aunt Alison could see it.

"Is that where the cave was?" I asked, recalling her story of the bats and the snakes.

"Not quite," said Aunt Alison. "That was in the mountain just to the east of Bison Rock. It was—" She paused, closing her eyes to think. "Maybe a half an hour east of here." She leaned over then to see out the window on the other side. "It was in an area we used to call Chapel Valley. I always thought the name had something to do with a chapel, but I learned later it was named for the

57

family who settled in it. In spite of the fact that I learned better, there's a part of me that's always thought chapels should be crescent-shaped!"

"Like that?" Aunt Alison's nurse asked, pointing out the window to something in the distance. Aunt Alison looked where the nurse pointed.

"Just like that," she said and from the way she said it, I knew we'd found it and it wasn't a parking lot at all. It was still a wild, untouched high meadow.

I scooted up to the pilot's cabin. We just had to have a close look. When I returned from the cockpit, Mother and Skye followed me back into Aunt Alison's section of the plane. They didn't want to miss this.

In a minute the plane banked and turned. Then we dipped down low and flew the curved length of Chapel Valley. It was everything I'd hoped for from the moment I'd asked Skye if we could do this.

"I remember!" Aunt Alison said breathlessly. "We used to stop and cool down in the shade of that big rock. That's where Lida dared me to go into the cave. Then, there, we tried to see into the cave from there, but we couldn't."

She started talking very fast then because she was racing with the airplane. "It was too dark to see, so we just had to go in. And there, by that tree, though it was barely a bush then. That's where we tied our horses up while we explored the cave. And there's the entrance to the cave. See it?!"

We all looked. We all could see. It was all so real I could almost see two girls hop off their ponies and approach the cave entrance.

Something happened then that I wouldn't have believed if I hadn't seen it with my own eyes. I don't know what caused it. Maybe it was the noise of the plane echoing down the valley. Maybe it was something else. I'll never know. All I do know is that at that exact moment a black dot appeared outside of the cave. It was followed by another and then another and the next thing any of us knew, the whole sky outside the cave entrance was filled with black dots, curving, swirling, dipping, flying. It was bats—thousands and thousands of bats.

Nobody said anything for the longest time, not until we were well clear of Chapel Valley. Then Aunt Alison spoke.

"I told you so."

There was a wonderful, totally satisfied grin on her face.

10

Mom and I left Los Angeles the next day. It had been a wonderful trip. I had had a great time with Skye, especially at Penelope's when I'd helped him out with his problems with Chris Oliver. But the best part of our L.A. vacation had to be meeting Aunt Alison again. With some help from my friend, Skye, I'd been able to do something for her that really made a difference. It wasn't going to change her health; I knew that. It was just going to relieve her of a regret. That's an important thing to be able to do for a friend.

As we flew home, I stared at the clouds, wishing that somebody could do that for me now. I still had one gigantic regret on my plate. I was about to lie to my best friends. For the first time since we'd formed The Saddle Club, I'd broken a promise to my best friends. Not only that, I was about to lie through my teeth about it.

PART II

Stevie's Summer

THIS HAS GOT to be the worst summer of my whole life. All my problems began when my three brothers built a tree house. At dinner one night, Dad got all misty-eyed about some tree house that he'd had when he was a kid and how the happiest memories of his boyhood all seemed tied to that tree house. No girls were allowed inside. Dad went on and on about how he and his best friends spent their finest hours there. You get the idea, I'm sure. Chad, he's my oldest brother, and Alex, he's my twin, got this idea that they should build a tree house for Dad for a birthday present. Michael, our youngest brother, said he'd like to help. I thought it was an okay idea and said they could count me in. What a mistake.

I didn't even have a chance to remind them that I got an A in woodworking (it was my only A that semester) before they all reminded me that Dad's tree house was "No Girls Allowed" and said that theirs was, too.

Both of our parents are lawyers so it's not unusual for us to draw on The Law in family disagreements. Naturally, I informed them that the Constitution guaranteed equal treatment of all. They reminded me that the Equal Rights Amendment hadn't passed. I tried to explain to them that it hadn't passed because the majority felt that the Constitution already guaranteed equality to women. The discussion went along in that vein for a while. Then it reverted to a screaming match and I took the opportunity to explain to each of my brothers just exactly how I really felt about them. There's no need for me to go into the specifics of what I said because it didn't work anyway. I wasn't going to be allowed into the tree house at any point— even during construction.

All through the week of summer vacation that it took the three of them to build the tree house, there was a big sign outside saying NO GIRLS ALLOWED. This is what my mother would call waving a red flag in front of an angry bull. In this case I'm the bull.

One night my brothers were all getting ready to go out to a baseball game with their scout troops. Nobody was near the tree house, so I climbed up to explore. I wasn't all that high, either. I have to confess that I thought it was a pretty neat tree house, though I'm sure my friends, Carole and Lisa, and I could build an even nicer one and I've got a tree in mind for just that purpose when I get better. As soon as my friends get back from their trips, I'm going to get them to do it. It'll be a good project for us since we can't go riding together the way we usually do, but I'm getting ahead of myself.

Just as I was trying to see how my brothers had made the walls so nice and snug, I heard voices down below. It was the three of them. Apparently they wanted to look at the tree house just one more time before they left for the game.

There was no way I'd let them have the satisfaction of seeing that I couldn't stay out of the tree house. I had to get out, but I couldn't go back out the door because my brothers were on that side, climbing up the ladder. Instead I went out a window on the other side of the tree house. I could see there was a tree branch right there and I thought maybe I could sit on it, sort of below the window.

It didn't work. I got out of the window and onto the branch all right, and I even straddled the branch. But that was the last thing that went right and it was partly my brothers' fault. They were jostling the tree as they climbed up and that jostled the branch I was sitting on.

Everybody dreams about how much fun it would be to slide down a bannister, right? Keep on dreaming about that, but don't *ever* dream about sliding down maple branches. It's not a dream, it's a nightmare. I slid all the way down—bannister style. I've been back to check it out since that day and I counted all the smaller branches, twigs, and shoots I slid over: twenty-seven. In about eighteen seconds, the place on me where I usually sit got severely bumped twenty-seven times! The final indignity was when I landed on the ground.

My brothers watched a lot of this from the tree house and have told everybody it was very funny. This will give you an idea of their idea of humor and it will show how obnoxious my brothers can be.

"She went *thud!* '*Yeooooowwwwwwwch!*' " Michael says, when he can tell the story without laughing too hard to get through it.

It wasn't funny. It hurt—really hurt. My hands were scratched, there were bruises on my legs, and my face was red where it had been slapped by a branch that popped up at me. Those all healed quickly. What didn't heal quickly was another part. The doctor called it a bone bruise on my coccyx. That's the part of the spine that would be a human's tail if we humans had tails. It's a part of your body you just never think about until it's not working right and mine doesn't work right, especially when it comes to sitting down.

There isn't much they can do for me. I got a pillow to sit on that's shaped like a donut. That's the polite way to describe it. When it comes right down to it, it bears a close resemblance to a toilet seat. This was pointed out to me by my brothers who think it's hysterically funny. As far as I'm concerned, they spend entirely too much time in the tree house, laughing at me and my pillow and thinking things are hysterically funny that aren't.

This all sounds pretty horrible, I know, but it's not even the worst of it. Sitting down is something a person can do without for a long time, unless that person happens to be horse-crazy. If you want to ride a horse, you've got to be able to sit down and there's nothing I like better than riding horses. I even like riding horses better than wreaking revenge on my brothers and that's a lot. And now I can't ride. I'm totally off horses for almost a month and I think it's the worst thing that has ever happened to me.

Now that I've told you how awful my brothers can be, and you're probably feeling sorry for me, there's a good side of this, too. My friends Lisa and Carole have been totally wonderful.

As soon as I got back from the doctor, I called both of them. We've got three-way calling on our phone and it's a lifesaver when it comes to The Saddle Club because it means we can have Saddle Club meetings even when we're not together. Before my parents got three-way calling, I'd spend the whole night on the phone talking with one or the other of my friends. Now I can spend the whole night on the phone, talking with both of them. It's perfect.

Anyway, I called them both and told them I'd hurt my bottom and I couldn't sit down.

"You mean you can't *ride*?!!" Carole said. Of course, she got it right away. So did Lisa.

"Oh, no, how are you going to get into a saddle?" Lisa asked.

I explained that I couldn't. We talked about how awful that was for a long time. See, it's very awful, so there was a lot to talk about.

The next day, we met at Pine Hollow. The two of them had convinced me that even if I couldn't ride, I could be around horses and besides, they wanted to see me. Since it's summer and we don't have school, we usually all go to the stable every day. It only makes sense, even if I couldn't ride.

The problem with going to Pine Hollow that morning was that I'd spent the whole time I was walking there thinking about how hard it was going to be to watch my friends ride when I couldn't. I could see Carole on Starlight, having a wonderful time as she worked on his training—and hers. And then there was Lisa, still working hard to catch up to learn as much as Carole and I know because Lisa started riding after we did. She was doing so well that I realized she might even catch up and pass me while I was grounded.

By the time I reached the stable, I was crying all over again. Carole and Lisa immediately hugged me and they took me into the grain storage room where nobody could see how awful I looked, or laugh at my pillow, or overhear our conversation.

My friends told me it was going to be okay and then they hugged me some more. That made me cry some more because it didn't seem to me that there was anything that could happen that would make it be okay.

"It just isn't fair that one of us can't ride," said Lisa.

"Right," said Carole. "If one of us can't ride, maybe none of us should be able to."

Lisa blinked a few times, then said, "Right."

That's how it happened. I swear it. I had nothing to do with it. They thought of it themselves.

I was still crying when Lisa turned to me and said, "I promise, Stevie, that as long as you can't ride, I won't ride."

"Me, too," said Carole.

That made me stop crying. I could hardly believe it. When I think back on it, it was the craziest thing any of us had ever done, but at the time, it seemed totally logical. My friends were trying to make me feel better and I've got to tell you, it made me feel better. How could anyone ask to have more generous friends than I do?

"It's a pledge from our hearts," Lisa said, putting her hand on her heart. She can be very dramatic sometimes.

"Absolutely," Carole promised.

Now, that would have been enough for me and I would have been glad to have it end there, but Lisa decided to carry it one step further. The next thing I knew they'd added an "or else" to the pledge. If any one of the three of us rode a horse before the doctor declared me well, that person would have to invite Veronica diAngelo to join The Saddle Club.

A word about Veronica diAngelo: *Bleaaaaaaaaa-uuugh!*

If, for a second, I had doubted my friends' sincerity about their pledge, all doubt was now gone. The very idea of inviting Veronica to join us was so horrible I knew neither one would break the pledge.

I couldn't imagine how they'd manage to do it, but over the next few days they each dropped a bomb. Lisa and her mother were going to Los Angeles to visit a sick aunt. Carole was going to New York with her father. That simplified the whole pledge thing for them. As long as they weren't going to be around horses, they wouldn't even be tempted!

The problem was that that left me all alone in Willow Creek, Virginia, with nothing to do.

"Don't be silly," Carole said in her most matter-of-fact, motherly voice. "Of course you've got lots of things to do. First of all, you can spend every day here, helping out. You know there's always a lot to be done with horses that you can do standing up."

"Sure," I said. "Then what's the second thing I can do?"

"Get into trouble!"

Lisa and Carole laughed at that one. I'll even admit that I did, too.

Later on, I figured out that Carole is a very wise girl, because I proceeded to do both of the things she'd suggested!

I NEED TO tell you a little bit about Max Regnery and his mother. They own and run the stable. We call Max by his first name and we call his mother Mrs. Reg. Max is our main riding instructor and he's a really great teacher. I can't say that about everybody who teaches me things (like don't get me started on my science teacher!), but Max is wonderful. He makes us work very hard and he doesn't take any nonsense. He won't even let us talk in class. I swear he can see out of the side of his head, too, because he can give instructions to three riders at once and he never makes a mistake about what they're doing wrong.

Mrs. Reg is the stable manager. She takes care of the business of the stable and that includes chores. Everybody at Pine Hollow is expected to work. We all tack up our own horses before we ride and then untack, groom, and water them when we're done. If Mrs. Reg catches anyone standing idle, the next thing they know, they've been handed a pitchfork and pointed toward a stall that needs mucking out.

When I realized I wasn't going to be able to ride for at least three weeks, I was afraid I'd spend the entire time mucking out stalls. It didn't turn out that way at all. I reported to Mrs. Reg for job assignments and she turned me right over to Max.

"Oh, Stevie! This is terrible!" Max said. Of course he understands how awful it is not to be able to ride. Then he got a look on his face that said that maybe this wasn't so bad after all.

"But if you can't work on your own riding skills, perhaps you'd like the opportunity to help others work on theirs."

"Huh?"

"First Session starts today. Would you like to help?"

During the summer, Max runs a day camp for riders. There are three two-week sessions, beginning with the youngest, most inexperienced riders and working up through the intermediates to the experts. They are all grouped by age rather than experience, though they tend to go together. First Session was for six- through eight-year-olds.

"You want me to be like a counselor?" I asked.

"Well, more like a counselor-in-training. I know it's

not the same thing as riding, but it's as close as you can get. And think about what good you'll be doing as a role model and helping our very newest, youngest riders to get the right start."

I could feel a grin coming. I'm a sucker for that kind of sales pitch.

"I'll try, Max. I'll really try," I said, and I meant it, too. "When a rider gets the right training from the very first, there's no limit to how far they can go, is there?"

"None whatsoever," Max assured me. "And as long as you stick to horses and stay out of trouble, you can be an enormous help."

That was when I figured out that Max was worried about the kinds of things I might do if I got bored. Naturally, it was in his best interest (and mine) to keep me busy.

"Come on with me now, Stevie, and meet the kids you'll be working with."

I followed him into the locker area. There was a whole group of cute little kids. They were chattering away, but stopped talking the second Max and I walked in. They looked at me curiously. I looked back at them curiously.

"Riders, I want you to meet my newest assistant, Stevie Lake." I got a kick out of that. "Stevie is one of my fine young advanced riders." I got an even bigger kick out of that. Max doesn't use a word like "fine" easily. "However, she's had an accident that makes it impossible for her to ride, at least for a while. So, while she's ground-bound,

75

she's going to help me and you. Listen to everything she says about horses, and you'll learn a lot."

At Pine Hollow, we're all expected to share our knowledge with everybody. Experienced riders are assigned to help those less experienced learn everything from tacking up to flying changes, so there was nothing new about being told to teach this group. What was new was the way they looked at me. With an introduction like that from Max, they gazed at me as if I were the smartest person in the whole world and would make their riding lessons the most fun they'd ever had. That was the biggest kick of all and I'll tell you what went through my mind when all of the kids looked at me. I thought: *I know more than they do.*

I suppose that sounds goofy, but the fact is, I'm a very competitive person. My boyfriend, Phil Marsten, is always telling me this. I knew some of the kids there, like May Grover, Jackie, and Amie. They were all in Horse Wise, our Pony Club. Naturally, they weren't the ones who needed the most help from me. I was working with the six-year-olds, the real new riders. They were totally cute.

There was one little girl named Leslie who I especially liked. Her mother had gotten her all new riding clothes— big enough to grow into. She was so cute you can't believe it. And she needed a lot of help. There were others, too. Max asked me to help Leslie, plus Natalie, Reuben, Mark, and Jessica. It only took us about forty-five minutes to get all their ponies saddled up and another ten to get them into the saddles and I've got to say, I loved every minute of it. The kids listened to everything I had to say and they learned. They really learned. Do you have any idea how wonderful it is to be able to share something as neat as riding with beginners? They weren't tall enough to put the saddles on the ponies' backs and they weren't strong enough to tighten the girths, but they wanted to know how to do it and they listened very hard. I liked that. Being the only girl with three brothers, it's sometimes hard for me to get listened to.

My group was just supposed to walk their ponies in circles and Max had me work with them in the indoor ring while he worked on more advanced things with the older kids. Once they'd walked around the ring six or seven times, I could tell they were eager to get onto something else. I knew Max would kill me if I let them trot, but there are a lot of things you can do at a walk so I started them on it.

For one thing, there's the jump position, also known as three-point position. It's called that because the rider is supposedly only in contact with the horse at three points —the ball of each foot touches a stirrup and the hands touch the horse's neck. It's really sort of standing up just a little bit from the saddle and it's a position you use a lot as part of other things—like posting, jumping, and sometimes cantering.

So, I got them all riding in three-point. When Max came into the ring and saw what I'd done, he was really pleased. The kids were thrilled at having learned something new and exciting and he was delighted that they were all doing it so well. Naturally, being Max, he had a lot of ideas on how to improve it.

"Reuben, put your heels down. You, too, Jessica. And, Natalie, you're too straight up. Lean forward a little bit. No, keep your back straight. Better. Yes! Mark, you should be looking straight ahead. Leslie, nice job. You've got it right!"

Then he turned to me. "You don't need me here anymore, do you?"

And that was just about the biggest compliment Max has ever given me!

As soon as Max left us, I decided I should teach the kids a game. We started playing a sort of Simon Says—only of course, I called it "Stevie Says." I couldn't do any complicated things with them, but I did have them stop, reverse directions, pat their ponies, rise to three-point—things like that. They thought it was fun and it also reminded them that they'd really learned some things their very first day in the saddle.

I was having fun *and* I was standing up. I even forgot about how much my injury hurt, until I tried to perch on the fence. I must have made a terrible face and I know I made a noise because everybody turned to look at me.

It's not easy explaining a bruised coccyx to a group of six-year-olds, but they were really nice and knew that it hurt me a lot. Leslie told me she knew a good doctor if I wanted one. She meant her father. Isn't that *cute?*

By the end of the day, I was exhausted. But it was a good kind of tired. I felt as though I'd accomplished a lot and that's a wonderful feeling. I walked home (no bike, of course) and as I went, every one of the kids passed me and waved.

"See you tomorrow!" they all called out.

I couldn't wait for morning to come.

THE FIRST THING I heard when I walked into the stable the next morning was Leslie saying, "Oh, Red!" and then giggling. That was even before I got to the ring. It seemed that Red O'Malley was teaching the group I'd thought of as "my" kids and it seemed that they'd already become "his" kids. I was about to offer to take over when Mrs. Reg called me into her office and explained that Red was too busy with the class to muck out the stalls today so she thought it would be a good idea for me to fill my idle hours with a pitchfork and a lot of manure.

I was on my third stall when Red and the kids arrived back in the stable.

"Oh, Red, that was so funny!" said Jessica.

"Yeah, you should have been there, Stevie!" said Natalie.

"Red's a *wonderful* teacher!" Leslie said. I could swear she sighed while she said it, too.

Like I cared!

Red helped all of the kids untack the ponies. They did it one by one, traveling in a pack. All the while that this was going on, I was mucking out Nickel's stall. That meant I was delivering loads of manure into a bucket, carrying it out to a pile, scraping the floor of the stall, lugging fresh straw and spreading it out in the stall. And then the minute Red brought Nickel into the stall, he produced a fresh load of manure. I know horses do that all the time and it doesn't mean anything at all, but at the time, it seemed like a perfect comment on the worth of all my work.

I was about to throw down the pitchfork when Max arrived.

"Red," he said. "I need you to ride out to the woods. Some riders reported that there was a coyote by the quarry. Can you head out there to see if there are any signs of it?"

"But Max, I'm about to demonstrate grooming techniques for this group."

"Stevie can do that just as well as you can," Max said, "and she can't ride out to the quarry. Right, Stevie?"

"Right, Max," I said. I was only too happy to put down the pitchfork (instead of throwing it down) and I was flattered that Max recognized my skills as a groom. Actually, they are legendary. I'm known throughout Pine Hollow as the best hoof picker in the place!

Red tacked up Diablo and headed for the woods. I cross-tied Penny in the stable aisle and pulled the hoof pick out of my pocket.

"The first thing you do when you begin grooming is to pick dirt and stones out of the horse's hooves." I held up the hoof pick. "I begin with the front feet, like this—" I showed them how you pat the horse above the leg and then you run your hand down his leg so he isn't surprised by the touch of your hand.

"It reassures them," I said.

"That's not the way Red did it when Reuben's horse was having a problem in class," said Natalie.

"Yeah, wasn't he funny?" Mark commented.

Leslie actually giggled, thinking back on whatever it was that Red had done.

"I wasn't there," I said. "I don't know why he did it differently, but this is the way *I* do it."

That doesn't sound very nice, I know, but I was annoyed. I followed my routine and picked the pony's hooves. Then I started the grooming.

There's a lot you can talk about while you're grooming a horse or a pony. You can talk about why it's good for the horse. You can talk about why they like it. You can talk about why you do all the things in a certain order, or you can talk about how often you do it or why you start at the horse's head and work backward or why sometimes the horses need reassurance and why sometimes they just stand still and love every second of it. There's plenty to say and I didn't say any of it. I just talked about Merlin.

"Every horse needs to be groomed. Every horse, that is, except Merlin."

"Who's Merlin?" Leslie asked. That was all the cue I needed.

"*What's* Merlin is a better question. Nobody's really sure whether he exists or not."

"Isn't Merlin King Arthur's magician?" asked Natalie.

"Maybe," I said. "Maybe he's something more, too. I mean I don't really know. Red told me not to say anything about Merlin to you. He didn't think you'd be interested. He's probably right." I know that wasn't fair to Red, but he'd been stealing my thunder and I just couldn't resist.

Before I said that, Reuben and Mark had been talking about how Penny swished her tail to get rid of flies. They stopped talking about Penny when I started talking about Merlin. Jessica had been gazing over to the refrigerator where her bag lunch was. She stopped gazing at that and started gazing at me. I just had to go on. Besides, not only am I the best hoof-picker at Pine Hollow, I'm hands down the best tall tale teller. I was just getting warmed up.

"Tell us more!" Leslie said. If I'd needed any more prodding, that was it. I told them more.

"If Merlin exists—and like I said, nobody's really sure about that—he lives in the forest."

"*This* forest?" Leslie asked, pointing out the window to the woods beyond the fields of Pine Hollow.

"Maybe," I said. "*If* he exists. Anyway, according to legend . . ." *Legend* is a word you should always use when you're telling a whopper like the one I was about to tell. It makes people think this story has been passed down from generation to generation and so it's *got* to be true. ". . . Merlin was brought to Willow Creek by the old woman who lived in the house on Garrett Road. You know that big old house on the hill?" That's another thing about tall tales. They work best if you tie them into something that everybody knows. This house was abandoned years ago and is about as creepy as a house gets. "They say the old woman was a witch—I don't know about that—only instead of riding around on her broomstick, she rode Merlin. That's how people knew when she was about to cast a spell—they could hear the steady clip-clop of his hooves!"

"The witch rode a horse?" Natalie asked. Her eyes were wide.

"Yes, a horse," I went on eagerly, "but not just any horse—a magical horse."

"What kind of spells did she cast?" Reuben asked.

"The *bad* kind," I said. "They say that all her spells had to do with horses. She loved Merlin so much and had so much fun riding him that she couldn't stand the idea that anybody else could have that kind of fun. One man had a young horse he really loved. She cast a spell that made

84

that young horse suddenly become a very old horse. The colt died of old age by the time he was three! Another time, there was a woman who loved to ride her horse at a canter. The woman cast a spell that made her get seasick so she couldn't stand the rocking gait of a canter anymore."

"Really?"

"That's what they say." I shrugged. "Everything she did made it impossible for people to ride."

"Like making somebody get a bruise on the place where they sit?" Leslie asked.

I hadn't even thought about that. I mean it. It hadn't occurred to me, but it was a really good idea.

"Maybe," I said.

"So what happened to the witch's horse?" Mark asked.

"Well," I replied. "Nobody's quite sure. According to the story that's told around town, there was one little girl who used to bring carrots to Merlin when he was in the paddock in back of the old woman's house. Merlin seemed to like her and the old woman couldn't stand that. It was bad enough that a horse made the little girl happy, but it was ten times worse that the horse was Merlin.

"One night, the woman climbed onto Merlin's back. She always rode bareback. It was Halloween, see, and the woman knew that the little girl would be going out in her costume and she was ready to cast her spell. She waited until the girl came to her house. She waited until the little girl got up to the door, and then the witch and Merlin rode like the wind—right up to the little girl. The woman swooped down, picked up the little girl, and took her to the woods. The little girl was terrified and whenever she asked the old woman what she was going to do, the old woman just said, 'Don't worry, little girl. You'll be fine. You just won't ever be able to ride a horse again in your whole life!' Then she cackled with glee."

I cackled for them then, too. I'm a pretty good cackler. I cackled so loudly that it made Leslie jump. I had them all frightened out of their wits. I'm so good it scares me sometimes.

"When they got into the darkest part of the woods— you know the stand of pines near the quarry"—they did, of course. The trees are very close together there and it's always dark, even at noon—"that's when the woman got off her horse and made the little girl stand in front of a tree while she cast her spell."

"What did the witch say?" asked Leslie.

"I don't know, but if I did, I wouldn't say the words. As soon as the witch had finished her incantation, the little girl started sneezing and wheezing. Then her eyes started itching and got all red. Then the tears began and she was sneezing even harder than before. The witch's spell had made her desperately allergic to horses! She was so miserable that the only thing she could do was to run from Merlin and the faster she ran, the harder the old woman laughed.

"Now, nobody's sure just exactly what happened next, but it appears that Merlin was very smart and understood what had happened and he wasn't happy about it because he loved the little girl. Since he didn't have any tack or even a lead rope, he took off—after the little girl. That made her sneeze all the harder and run all the faster. But she was in the dark woods, at night. The inevitable happened. She tripped on something and fell down and Merlin caught up with her."

"Didn't she get sicker?"

"At first, she did. You're right, but remember, Merlin is a magical horse so then the magic began. The little girl always said she never actually heard anything, but she swore that horse talked, uttering a chant, an incantation, and when he was done, she didn't sneeze anymore."

"Magic?" Natalie asked.

"That's what they say. Then Merlin sort of waited for her and the little girl just knew she could trust the horse. She climbed onto his back. Some people say the horse cantered back to town. Others say he flew. Nobody but the little girl knows for sure and she's not telling. What the world does know is that the little girl turned out just fine and never sneezed at another horse again. Nobody ever saw the old woman on Garrett Road again."

"What about the horse?"

"They say he lives in the deep piney woods and whenever somebody there loves horses, Merlin knows. And if they need his help, he'll be there for them. On the dark nights when the wind blows and the shadows dance on the forest floor, some people say the shadows are branches. Others say they're horse tails. Me? I don't know."

"Wow!" said Leslie.

She loved that story. So did the other kids. They hadn't thought about Red O'Malley from the moment I'd started talking.

THE NEXT MORNING started off okay. In spite of my sore you-know-what, I'd had a pretty good night's sleep so at least until I got downstairs for breakfast, things were looking up.

Then came the day's first piece of bad news. It was my mom's annual You-can't-have-a-good-day-unless-you-start-with-a-good-breakfast attempt to improve the world. That means oatmeal in case you can't figure it out. Then, as I was staring at the globulous mess, Mom handed me two pieces of mail and for once neither of them was addressed to "Or Current Resident." They were both for me and they were postcards from Lisa and Carole, arriving from opposite coasts on the very same day.

Much as I wanted to hear everything my friends had to tell me, I didn't want to get all the good news with the bad news of the oatmeal, so I stuck them in my pocket, explained to Mom that I was too full from dinner to eat the oatmeal, and dashed out of the house to get to Pine Hollow before she could corner me with another lecture on the benefits of iron and fiber.

When I arrived, Max was just giving final instructions to the older riders about the trail ride they were going to take in the woods. Red and I were to be in charge of the littler kids again. That was basically okay except for the fact that I love trail rides more than anything. Max knows it, too. I actually think he was trying to get the riders out of there before I arrived so I wouldn't feel so bad about having to miss it, but it didn't work. I saw everything and I was really envious of what they were about to do. That, combined with the oatmeal, made me feel sort of overwhelmed. I was watching the older riders leave for their trail ride when Red came up to me.

"Uh, Stevie, can I make you a deal?"

"Like what?"

"Like this morning, I'm going over tacking and untacking with the beginners. After I'm done with that, I've got a dentist appointment at lunchtime. So, my deal is that I'll do the tacking demonstration if you'll look after the kids at lunch. I shouldn't be more than an hour and a half. That'll give you time to eat and then begin the mucking demonstration."

Mucking demonstration! So much for all the good I did teaching the kids three-point riding. I'd already been demoted to mucking demonstrations. This did not make me happy. Instead it made me think about eating oatmeal for breakfast and receiving postcards from my lucky friends who got to go to glamorous places.

"Sure, Red. Whatever you say."

See how agreeable I can be even when I'm not feeling it?

That seemed like as good a time as any to read my postcards. I needed a little peace and quiet. The older riders were off in the woods; Red and the young riders were in the stable. I walked through the stable and out to the paddock where there was one horse standing in the summer sun.

When you're in a paddock, there's only one place to sit down and that's on a fence. Without thinking, I ootched up to the top of it. (Ootching is what I call it. It's sort of a backward climb using the heel of your boots to give you leverage on the fence boards.) Then I perched on the top of the fence, just like I always do. Later, they said my scream could be heard three towns away, but I think they were exaggerating. I'd just forgotten about the fact that my bottom had the bone bruise and when I sat on the fence, it really hurt. Red and the kids came running out of the stable to see what had happened. This was a case of crying leading to laughing because I had tears of pain rolling down my cheeks and Red thought it was hilariously funny.

That was the meanest, most thoughtless thing he'd

ever done and I told him so. I screamed at him. I was about as angry as I get—and I get pretty angry. "I've got this awful wound in a totally unmentionable place and you think it's funny! I can't sit down or lie down or even ride a horse. For all I know, it'll never get better and I'll never be on a horse again!"

I sometimes have what people refer to as a "flair for the dramatic," which is a nice way of saying I exaggerate. I knew I'd ride again, but it had been almost a week since I had and it was going to be a lot more weeks until I could and I've got to say, it felt like a lifetime.

Anyway, Red must have gotten my point because he told me he was sorry and said I should relax and take a little time to myself—as if that hadn't been exactly what I'd been trying to do. He went back into the stable. I climbed up on the fence again and perched very carefully and read the cards from Lisa and Carole. They should have made me feel better, but they didn't.

The problem was that my friends were having wonderful times and they told me so. Lisa had been out to dinner with Skye Ransom! That's every girl's dream come true. Don't get me wrong. I was happy for Lisa, all right, but I was unhappy for me. Things didn't improve when I learned that Carole was having a blast in New York.

Never mind the Skye Ransom part. Just think how you'd feel if one of your two best friends was in glamorous Los Angeles and the other one was in exciting New York, and you were stuck in Willow Creek!

I carefully got down off the fence and walked back through the paddock. I needed to be someplace by myself and somehow it didn't seem right for me to be in a beautiful place like the paddock when I was feeling so gloomy. I sneaked into the stable, climbed up the ladder to the loft, and lay down in a soft pile of hay.

I probably went to sleep. I was only vaguely aware of voices downstairs. First of all, Red was droning on and on about how to put tack on a pony. Then there were other sounds and I might possibly have heard Red yell upstairs about leaving. I'm being as honest as I can and I've got to tell you that I'm just not sure about that one. I was vaguely aware of the sounds of the younger riders fetching their lunches from the refrigerator and then I could hear them talking. I should have gone down to be with them, but by then I was definitely asleep because I was having this wonderful dream about riding on a movie set in New York with Skye Ransom. My dream was much more interesting than anything the little kids were saying.

Anyway, the first thing I really remember is nothing. That's an odd way to put it, but that was what I thought of when I opened my eyes. There was nothing. No sounds at all.

A stable is usually a pretty noisy place. The horses stomp, snort, whinny, and neigh. And the riders make all sorts of sounds, especially little kids who are prone to shrieks. No sounds means no riders and no horses and when I realized that, I knew for sure that something was wrong.

I sat up and looked at my watch. It was 12:30. That meant that the kids should have been having a quiet time after lunch, but not *that* quiet. The silence meant there were no horses and no ponies in the stable at all.

Mrs. Reg was running errands; Max was on a picnic with the older riders; Red was at the dentist. That meant I was in charge, but where were my charges and where were their ponies? That was the question I had to answer right away.

WHEN THINGS ARE going wrong, my mind can race pretty fast. So can I. I slid down that ladder so fast I picked up three splinters and I never even noticed them until the next day!

"Hey, kids! Where are you?"

Dumb question. If nobody's there, nobody can answer. It didn't get any better with the next question.

"Ponies? Are you around? Hello????"

See what I mean. Like I said, though, I'm being honest here so you might as well know *all* the dumb things I did.

I thought maybe they might have let the ponies out into one of the exercise rings. Nope. One of the paddocks? Nope. The indoor ring? Nope. The field? I climbed up on one of the fences to see as far as I could. There was no sign of them.

About this time, it occurred to me that if the kids had gone someplace on horseback, they'd need to have their ponies tacked up so I checked the tack room. That's when it really hit me. All of the ponies' tack was gone. That meant, beyond a shadow of a doubt, that the kids were riding the ponies and since I couldn't see where they were, they had to be far away and if they were far away, I was in big trouble. Even worse, they could be, too.

I love trail rides of all kinds, but you've got to know what you're doing to take a horse beyond the limits of a riding ring and these kids were just beginners. Not only that, they were just beginners who couldn't possibly be strong enough to tighten their ponies' girths enough to ride safely. The first thought that entered my mind was an image of Leslie falling off her pony. It wasn't a pretty sight and it scared me more than anything else that had happened in the previous five minutes since I'd awakened in the hayloft.

If the riders weren't in the paddocks and the fields around Pine Hollow, they had to be in the woods somewhere. That's when I remembered Max asking Red about the coyote near the quarry. The image that came into my mind then was even worse than Leslie's just being thrown.

I knew there was a possibility that absolutely nothing was going wrong and the kids were just having fun in the woods. I also knew that there were too many possible dangers for me to think of counting on that. I had to get to them.

But how?

It was while I was pondering that question that I went into the locker area and saw the note they'd left. It was even worse than I'd thought.

> Stevie—We've gone to find Merlin for you. You need his magic so you can ride horses again!
> See you later! On horseback!

I promise that's the last tall tale I'm ever telling in my whole life!

The woods are on the far side of the fields. It's about a half-mile ride to the edge of the woods and then there are miles and miles of trails. Lisa, Carole, and I never think much about the distances because we only ever do it on horseback. At a trot, a horse reaches the woods in a few minutes. On foot, wading through the grass, it would take me twenty. Then, once I reached the woods, I'd be even worse off because there are so many choices, though I'd go to the quarry first and that was about two miles into the woods—another forty-five minutes on foot.

The choices were not exactly great. I could take hours and hours on foot to accomplish exactly nothing, or I could ride. On horseback, it'd be a cinch to find them within about a half hour, no matter where they were, especially if I rode Topside, who could run like the wind.

If I could sit down.

But that was the point, wasn't it? I couldn't sit down? On the other hand, I didn't have a choice about riding; I had to do it. There are some things that can be done on horseback better than any other way and looking for riders in the woods was one of them. I *had* to ride.

That decided, I worked on how I was going to do it. The answer was staring me in the face because I'd been working on it very hard with the young riders just a short time before. I would ride in the three-point position. It would tire my legs, but tiring my legs was a lot better than bruising my seating area any further. I didn't waste any more time.

I grabbed Topside's tack, took him out of his stall, led him to the entrance to the stable, and mounted—very carefully. Once I had both feet in the stirrups, I did the most sensible thing I'd done in days: I touched the good-luck horseshoe. Now was the time when I needed good luck more than I'd ever needed it before, and not just for myself.

I clucked my tongue against the roof of my mouth, nudged Topside with my calves, and we were off.

I'VE ALWAYS THOUGHT Topside was the smartest horse in the world. I only have to tell him things once and he gets the idea and does it even better than I would have told him to do it if I'd had to tell him a second time. We soared across the fields, stopping only very briefly to open gates and then close them behind us. No matter how bad an emergency is, it can only be made worse by leaving gates open.

In spite of what you may think of me based on what you've already learned, I'm a pretty practical person—though not as practical as Lisa—and my practical side told me to assume the worst and head for the quarry, where the biggest trouble could lie.

Although I was very worried about the kids and I was worried about my ability to ride for an extended period of time in the standing-up position and even more worried about how much it would hurt if I made a mistake and sat down, I was not so worried about any of those things that I couldn't appreciate what a wonderful time I was having riding Topside.

Luckily for me, Topside has marvelous gaits. He took up a trot that lifted his silky black mane from his neck in the wind and that sped us across the field. When the way seemed clear, I signaled for a canter and we took off. The scents of warm sunshine and fresh grass mingled with the rich, pungent smell of Topside and his leather tack. Breezes brushed against my cheek. The landscape rushed by. After so many days without riding it felt wonderful.

It also made me think of Lisa and Carole and how much I wished they could have been there with me, both to appreciate how wonderful it was to ride and to help me with the little kids just in case they were in trouble.

Something nagged at my conscience right then, but I was enjoying myself too much to wonder what it was. It would come back to me later, I knew.

When we entered the woods, we slowed to a trot and then a walk as the path became narrower and more rocky. I'd spent hours in the woods with Lisa and Carole and I knew every nook and cranny of every trail. I headed for the piney woods near the quarry, where I'd made the witch cast her spell and where I'd told the kids they might find Merlin. I knew they wouldn't find Merlin. I *hoped* they wouldn't find a coyote.

Topside climbed the last hill approaching the quarry and then slowed and stopped as if he wanted to listen. His ears perked up and pointed around, like periscopes. Horses have very good hearing and if Topside was listening, I knew I needed to listen, too.

I heard crying. It sounded like someone was hurt, and it was coming from over the top of the hill, right near the quarry. My worst fears were being realized.

"I'm coming!" I yelled and then I gave Topside such a nudge that he was startled into action. He got the message, sensing my urgency, and he was up and over the hillside in a matter of seconds.

"I'll be right there! Hold on! Wait for me!" I called, sending my voice ahead, hoping to give some reassurance to the child in trouble.

What I saw when we crested the hill will stay in my mind forever, along with the feeling of worry, shame, and embarrassment about my own part in what had happened. The kids were all on the far side of the quarry. Leslie was sitting on the ground, crying. Reuben and Natalie were standing next to her. There was no sign of any of their ponies. Mark and Jessica were still on their ponies, but just barely. Jessica's saddle was slipping off to the left. Mark was having trouble controlling Penny and was clutching her mane for dear life.

"I'll be right there," I called across the quarry. "Don't do anything, okay?"

It took me and Topside a few minutes to get over to the

other side of the quarry. I only remember thinking how relieved I was to know that the kids were okay—if you didn't count Leslie's knee. I don't even remember wondering about the three missing ponies. As long as the kids were safe, everything else was going to work out, right?

7

ALL FIVE KIDS started talking at once. Four, actually, because what Leslie did was to cry some more.

"Stop, stop, stop!" I said, dismounting as carefully as I'd mounted in the first place. I secured Topside's reins to a tree and then knelt as best I could beside Leslie to take a look at her knee.

It was okay. She just needed to know that.

"Oh, boy, I know that hurts, Leslie, but you're going to be all right."

"I am?"

"Sure. I've had worse."

"You have?"

"Well, there was the time I thought it would be a neat idea to let our dog pull me along the sidewalk when I was on roller skates. . . ."

Leslie got the picture and made a face.

"The good news about that was that I did a job on both of my knees and it was so bad I charged kids twenty-five cents to take a look. I don't think this is going to be worth more than a dime."

She laughed. That made me feel better. It made her feel better, too.

"Look, the creek runs right over there. Natalie, take Leslie over to it and see if you can rinse away some of the dirt. We'll give you a good cleanup when we get back to Pine Hollow, but for now, this'll do, okay?"

Natalie helped Leslie stand up, held her arm across her shoulder, and the two of them walked slowly toward the creek. I turned to take care of the next problem—Jessica.

"Don't do anything right now, Jessica," I said as I walked over toward her. "If you move any more, you'll shift your weight and the saddle will go the whole way. Stay steady. Hold the reins firmly. Not too tight."

I kept talking and she kept listening. She just froze in place. The pony, whose name was Dime, wasn't any more comfortable with the saddle shifted to the side than Jessica was. He didn't move, either. I stood next to Dime, offered my arms to help Jessica down, and she took the offer. The instant she was out of the saddle, the whole thing slipped all the way, and hung there, upside down. I hated to think what would have happened if Jessica were still aboard.

"The same thing happened to Nickel!" Reuben said.

That explained Leslie's fall, but it didn't explain why we had five riders and only two ponies.

"As soon as Leslie fell, Natalie and Reuben got down off their ponies to help her. The ponies just ran off!" Jessica said. "Maybe they were scared by Leslie's crying."

"I don't blame them. Do you?" I asked.

That made Jessica laugh.

"Nope," she agreed. "Dime almost did the same thing, but I held on."

"Me, too," said Mark.

I could see then that his knuckles were white from holding on to his pony's mane. He hadn't relaxed one bit since I'd arrived and the pony, Half Dollar, was looking a little annoyed.

I checked to see whether his girth was tight enough and found that it only needed tightening two notches. Then I assured him he was safe and could let go.

"I can?"

"Try it," I said. He did and it worked. I was awfully glad to know that a horse's mane doesn't have any nerves in it so his tight clutching hadn't hurt the pony at all. Half Dollar did shake his head, though, relieved to be released. I smiled and gave the good old boy a pat. Mark patted him, too.

Next I righted Dime's saddle, adjusted the blanket, and tightened the girth. He was ready to go again and I was pretty sure Jessica would be ready to get on him in just a few minutes.

By then, Leslie and Natalie were returning from the creek and the next thought occurred to Leslie.

"But where are *our* ponies?" she wailed. That started another sprouting of tears.

"Calm down," I said. "Horses can run off, but they rarely run far. You guys just wait here and I'll be right back, okay? Actually, I could use a hand. Mark, Jessica, could you come with me?"

Jessica looked at Dime a little unsurely, but she was tough. She climbed back into the saddle, just the way I'd taught her only a few days before. She looked at me and said, "Ready."

It made me very proud of her. It's not easy to have an uncomfortable experience on a horse (and a sideways saddle is about as uncomfortable as it gets) and then to climb back into the saddle. The girl had guts. Mark, holding just the reins, no mane, said, "Me, too." Mark had guts, too.

I climbed back into Topside's saddle—well, a good three inches above it, but you know what I mean—and we were off.

It turned out that that was the easiest part of the day. I was right about the ponies not running very far, but the best news was that they were all together. Horses and ponies are social animals with a herding instinct. When they aren't following a human's instructions, they'd just as soon be with other horses. All three of them were in a small open area of the forest, nibbling at fresh greens just as if nothing bad had ever happened. We rode up to them.

"Here's how you lead a horse while you're on horseback," I said, handing Jessica a set of reins to hold. She did it very well. So did Mark. The ponies seemed a little relieved to be told what to do and stopped their nibbling right away. I dismounted and straightened out Nickel's saddle. He nickered when I got it on right, indicating that it had been as uncomfortable as it looked. Then I got back in (above) Topside's saddle and we returned to the quarry with the ponies in tow.

"Oh, Nickel, you're all right!" said Leslie. She limped over to him and gave him a big hug. I knew I wasn't going to have any trouble getting her back in the saddle when we were ready to go!

Natalie and Reuben each took their pony's reins and then I showed all of the kids how to secure a horse or a pony so they wouldn't run off.

"It's a really bad idea to use the reins," I explained. "You're always supposed to use a lead rope so you don't damage the reins and so the bit won't move every time the horse moves. Still, it's a whole lot better to use the reins than to use nothing!"

"I guess we learned that already," said Reuben sheepishly.

"I guess you did," I agreed. "Now let's see what else you've learned."

I had in mind to have a little talk with them to be sure

they were all calm before we headed back to Pine Hollow. So, once I was sure all the ponies and Topside were well secured, I perched on the edge of a rock in the quarry and the kids all sat down with me.

"Are you angry with us?" Leslie asked.

"Angry? No. I'm just relieved to know you're all okay. I should have been there with you. I had no business leaving you all alone when Red left. You guys should be angry with me. Aren't you?"

"Nope," said Mark. The rest nodded, agreeing.

"Well, since nobody's angry, maybe we can just take a minute here to get a few things straight." I was putting on my teacher voice. I've heard enough teacher lectures in my life to know just how to do it.

"Trail riding is something experienced riders can do without an instructor. It's something intermediate riders can do *with* an instructor and it's something novice riders —that's you guys—can't do at all."

"But we did it, didn't we?" Reuben said smartly.

There was something about him that reminded me of myself.

"Yes, you did it, and look what trouble it got you into!" I was very aware of sounding like Miss Fenton, the principal of my school. I'm not proud of it, either, but I persisted. "What on earth were you all thinking of when you decided to do this?"

"You," Leslie said simply.

"Yeah. We wanted to find Merlin for you," said Natalie.

"We heard what you said to Red about never being able to ride again and, well, we just thought, maybe . . ."

My face turned red. This whole thing was my fault. "Look, guys," I said. "That's just pretend. There's no such thing—"

"But you told us the whole story!" said Natalie.

"*Story*. That's what it was. A story. There's nothing to it. There never has been."

"It's a *legend*," said Leslie. "Everybody knows that there's always some truth to a legend."

"Not this one," I said. "I made up the whole legend right then and there in the stable yesterday. There never was a witch; she never had a horse."

"But there's the house on Garrett Road . . ." Leslie reminded me.

"Well, there's a North Pole, too, but do you really think that a red-suited man lives there, makes toys, and trains flying reindeer?"

The look on Reuben's face indicated that he at least sort of *hoped* that one was true.

"Reuben?"

"Nah, I know better, really."

"And do you know better now than to believe in a witch and a magical horse?"

"Maybe," he said. "Yeah, maybe it's true and you just don't know it." There was that side of him again.

"Right. Did you ever think of that?" Leslie piped in.

Mark, Natalie, and Jessica started nodding, as though they were agreeing with Reuben and Leslie.

I stood up and put my hands on my hips. I knew they were young and all, but I couldn't help feeling surprised that any one of them could actually believe in the tall tale I'd told them.

"I made it up. I fabricated it from thin air," I said impatiently. "I should have been telling you all about grooming and instead, I invented a story about a magical horse who never was and never will be and who doesn't have any magic."

"I'm not so sure about that. Not only is there magic, but it works!" Jessica said, siding completely with Reuben and Leslie and utterly confounding me.

"And just what would lead you to believe that there is any such magic?" I asked.

Leslie cocked her head and looked at me slyly. "Well, you're riding, aren't you?"

For the first time since I'd gathered the young riders around me, I was speechless.

By the time we got back to Pine Hollow, my mind was more of a mess than it had been when I'd left. In fact, the only good news I could think of was that except for Leslie's knee, the kids were unharmed and the ponies were safe. For my own part, my legs were killing me from standing up in the saddle for so long and even worse, my sitting-down section had hit Topside's saddle enough for me to know I'd put my own recovery back a couple of weeks. It wasn't going to matter, though. When Max learned that I'd let the kids go on a trail ride without an instructor, he was never going to let me near a horse again, with or without a sore bottom.

"Stevie?" It was Reuben interrupting my miserable thoughts.

"Yup?"

"We've just figured out that we've gotten you into big trouble, haven't we?"

"I think I did most of the work on that myself, Reuben. You kids aren't responsible. I'm just irresponsible."

"Maybe, but isn't Max going to be angry with you?"

"I think we can count on that."

"And he ought to be angry with us."

"I think you can count on that, too," I said. "Actually, he won't be angry so much as worried, but sometimes worry comes out as anger. I bet each of you can count on your parents for both worry and anger, too."

"I don't want my mother to be worried and angry," Leslie said.

"Me, neither," added Mark.

"That's a lot of worry and anger," said Reuben.

"And a lot of upset adults," I said. "Too much worry and anger isn't good for them, but life is like that sometimes. It's called facing the music." Frankly I was tired of life lessons for the day, but there was another one staring me in the face.

"Hmmmmm," said Jessica.

"Look! There's Max! He's waving at us!"

He was, too. I could see him standing next to the paddock behind Pine Hollow, waving widely. We all waved back. I think the kids thought he was welcoming us home. I sort of thought it was more like, "Get yourselves in here before you're grounded for life!" Since none of the kids could trot, we just walked slowly and carefully—me still standing tall in the saddle.

When we arrived and dismounted, I told the kids to take their ponies to their stalls and said I'd be in in a minute to help them. I deserved the tongue-lashing; they didn't.

"Max, I'm sorry," I began.

He interrupted me as well he should. Nothing I was going to say was going to be anywhere near as bad as what he had to say, so he had to have a chance to say it and I had to listen to it.

"Stevie, the minute I got back here and saw Topside and the ponies gone, I knew exactly what had happened."

"You did?" I mean, how could he have known about Merlin?

"Of course it was only going to take you a couple of days to figure out that you could ride standing up and the minute you figured it, you were going to be in the saddle. I'm not dumb. I can't say I'm happy about your taking the kids out without an adult, but I guess I can't blame you for wanting to do it. It was awfully hard for you to watch us leave today. The look on your face this morning said it all."

"Max, I—"

"Look, there's really no excuse for doing what you did, but if there were one, it would be the one you have—"

"Max, you don't—"

"But I really do, Stevie. I do understand how much

horses and riding mean to you. I do understand how much you love it and how hard it is to not be able to do it. I do. I can't condone your taking those young riders out on a trail ride without an adult, but I can understand it. Really. Even though I can see that Leslie's had an accident."

"Max, you're being too nice."

Can you believe I said that? It's a sign of how upset I was by what I'd done and how astonished I was by what Max had assumed I'd done.

"No, Stevie, I'm not going to be all that nice. Much as I understand it, I can't let you get away with it free and clear. There have to be consequences for irresponsible behavior."

"I know," I said.

"So, even though you've figured out how to ride with a sore seat, I'm going to ground you for the rest of this session. No riding. Period. I still need you as a helper, but I can't let you get on a horse."

The thing Max couldn't know—and which I had no intention of discussing with him—was that my bottom was so sore from the little bit of sitting I'd had to do in the saddle that there was no way I could possibly have gotten into the saddle for the next two weeks.

He had more to say and the news was just as good. "Moreover, I want you to know that in no way do I blame the kids for this. They are not going to hear one word of it from me. You can explain to them why you aren't riding anymore."

"I'll take care of it, Max," I promised, realizing that I'd miraculously managed to take on one hundred percent of the blame and best of all, the kids wouldn't be punished.

"I want you to take care of Leslie's knee, too. You know where the bandages are. I'll talk with her mother and explain. Are we done?"

Were we ever! "Yes, Max. And, uh, again, I'm sorry."

"I know you are. I really do understand."

He didn't, of course, but that was okay. I couldn't have asked for a better outcome and I was almost walking on air as I led Topside back to his stall and said good-bye to him for two weeks (except for grooming him and watering him and mucking out his stall and tacking him up for other riders, etc., etc.). Really, the only bad news was that Carole and Lisa weren't there to share my triumph. They always say I have a way of getting away with murder and though this wasn't exactly murder, it was the next closest thing in Pine Hollow terms—and I *was* getting away with it, practically scot-free!

Once I secured the latch on Topside's stall, I went to the section where the ponies were kept. It was all I could do to keep a grin off my face and when I found the kids, I gave them all one big hug.

"What did Max say?" Leslie asked.

"He thinks I took you out on the trail ride because I was so happy that I'd figured out how to ride again."

"Is that what you told him?" Reuben asked, sounding

admiring. Clearly, he'd decided that was a pretty clever lie.

"Actually, no. I was about to tell him what happened, but when Max assumed something different, well, I couldn't honestly see any reason to make things look worse than they are. I know it's sort of a lie. . . ."

"But it doesn't make us look as stupid as the truth does, does it?" That was Reuben.

"If you want to put it that way," I conceded.

"So, what's going to happen to us?"

"To you, nothing. To me, well, I'm grounded for two weeks."

"You mean you have to stay home?" Leslie asked. I was touched by her concern.

"No, it means I have to come here and work with the horses, but not ride."

"Oh, well, that's not soooooo bad," she said.

"No, it's not soooooo bad," I agreed. "I can live with it. It seems like mild punishment for what I actually did. And the other thing I have to do is help you clean up that cut and bandage it."

I took her hand and led her to Mrs. Reg's office to get the medicine and bandages and then to the big double sink where we could clean it.

Leslie took off her boot and rolled up her pant leg very carefully. I could see that the cut hurt and I knew we'd both feel better when we got it covered.

I ran the water and got some clean cloths and soap. We rinsed it in warm water and then washed it very carefully.

"Natalie and I did a good job in the creek," she said. "That was smart of you to suggest it."

"All from experience," I assured her. "When you're out in the woods, you sometimes have to improvise."

"What does that mean?"

"Make up stuff."

"Like ghost stories?"

"Not exactly. It means more like making do with what you've got. You had to wash the cut. There wasn't any soap and warm water, but there was cool water and I know the creek is clean because it comes from hills where there isn't any pollution, so it was only logical."

"That's what you are, Stevie, you're very logical."

It was a compliment and I appreciated it, but there was something about her use of the word "logical" that caused a tingle in my memory banks. I ignored it for a few minutes while I finished tending to the knee.

Once the cut was washed, I dried it very carefully, then I put some ointment on the bandage and applied it to the knee, taping it in a way that wouldn't cut off circulation, but that would stay on. It looked pretty professional and Leslie hadn't grimaced once, so I must have done a good job.

She brought her pant leg down again over the bandage, put her sock back on, and then tugged her boot back over it. Aside from the hole in her new riding pants, she looked very put-together. I looked at her and smiled. She smiled back, a sweet innocent smile. Suddenly she seemed so young, even though she had on very grown-up-looking riding clothes: fawn-colored pants, shiny black boots, snowy white blouse, black riding jacket. All those brand-new clothes only made me think of one thing: Veronica diAngelo.

I gasped and then I gagged as the full impact of what had happened that day hit me, smack in the face.

I'd been on a horse. I'd ridden a horse. My friends and I had pledged that we wouldn't ride. I, of all people, had violated the pledge.

I had a good excuse, I knew, but no excuse was good enough in the face of a pledge to my two best friends. We'd made a promise to one another and nothing Max would ever know or not know about what had really happened was going to make a difference when it came to Carole and Lisa. Friends don't lie to one another so I would have to tell them. But then, if I told them, it would mean we'd have to invite Veronica to join The Saddle Club. Correction, it would mean *I* would have to invite Veronica. If I did that, Carole and Lisa would never speak to me again and what would be the point of having The Saddle Club if they wouldn't speak to me again.

I had two choices: I could lie to my friends, which was unthinkable, or I could tell them and invite Veronica to join, which was unthinkable.

"Oh, Stevie! My knee doesn't hurt at all. I really believe there is magic. Everything's worked out so well!"

Leslie gave me a big hug and I had to hug back. It wasn't her fault that she was all wrong. She couldn't know that there wasn't any magic at all, or if there was magic, it was just black magic—the kind witches use. But there I go again, and I was done telling tall tales.

Or was I? I had two weeks to decide.

PART III

Carole's Summer

I LOVE DRIVING places with my father. There's something so nice about it's being just the two of us alone, no phone, no television, no interruptions. We've had a lot of time together alone at home since Mom died, but being in the car is somehow special.

Dad and I were on our way to New York. We live in Virginia, so it's about a five-hour drive to New York City, where we were going to spend a couple of weeks. Ordinarily I wouldn't have been thrilled about spending so much time away from Pine Hollow, the stable where I ride and board my horse, Starlight. But for once being far from horses actually appealed to me.

Once we were on the Interstate, Dad asked me about it —right after he'd found the oldies station on the radio.

He would have asked me sooner, but they were playing "There's a Moon Out Tonight" and he had to sing along. He's got a good voice. I didn't mind at all. I even joined in on some of the falsetto parts. We're good together.

"I'm glad you're here," he said.

"Me, too."

Then he reached over and squeezed my hand. I squeezed back. That was one of his ways of saying that being in a car with me was as special for him as it was for me.

"You've been in New York before, haven't you?"

"Sure, with Max, Mrs. Reg, and Stevie and Lisa." I was talking about my riding instructor and his mother, and of course my two best friends in The Saddle Club. "We went to the horse show."

"And you rode in Central Park, didn't you?"

"Yup. And that's where we met Skye Ransom. We taught him to ride, you know." Skye Ransom is this incredibly cute movie star, but you know that already, don't you?

"That's right," Dad commented. "Well, I'm glad you're coming with me this time, but I *am* wondering what changed your mind. Two days ago, you said there was no way you could leave Pine Hollow Stable and your wonderful horse Starlight for a couple of weeks. Is Starlight all right? I mean he's not lame or anything, is he? You'd tell me, wouldn't you?"

"Starlight's fine, Dad; it's Stevie who's got a problem."

Dad gave me a quizzical look that indicated the statement I'd just made didn't make any sense. If you think about it, it probably doesn't, but any sentence with the name "Stevie" in it is likely to be confused. She's that kind of girl. I explained to Dad about Stevie's sitting area and how it got hurt falling out of a tree house.

Dad started laughing by the time I described Stevie crouching outside the window of the house high up in the tree. Honestly, I never thought it was all that funny, but then Stevie's a really good friend of mine. What am I saying? She's a really good friend of Dad's, too. The two of them both adore stuff from the fifties and sixties. Last year, Dad threw his back out trying to play with a Hula-Hoop Stevie gave him for his birthday. They both love awful jokes, too. So, why was Dad laughing?

"I can just see her!" he said between snorts. "I bet she was madder than a hornet that her brothers tried to keep her out of the tree house. I mean, I'm glad she didn't get hurt worse, but sliding all the way down the branch!"

"But, Dad, she *did* get hurt worse! She got a bone bruise on her coccyx. Do you know where that is?"

"Of course I do," he said. "It's where you sit down."

"Like in a *saddle*," I said, emphasizing the word.

"Oh, no." He understood.

The radio then played "Heartbreak Hotel," which

seemed quite appropriate to me. Dad had to sing it, too. I let him do a solo. When it was over, I went on.

"So, Lisa and I pledged that we wouldn't ride horses until Stevie could. It made her feel a lot better. And I don't mind, really."

"As long as you can come to New York with me?"

"Well, the timing did seem good," I admitted.

"And who's going to exercise Starlight while you're gone?"

"Red O'Malley. Max has the first session of summer camp going on and Red will be riding a lot while he instructs the young kids. He can use Starlight whenever he wants. It'll free up the rest of the stable horses for other riders. It seemed like a good deal."

"Hmmmmm." That's a phrase my father uses occasionally when he's got something on his mind that he has to think about, but he's not ready to talk about. I knew I'd have to wait.

I waited through two Motown hits and a Sam Cooke ballad. We then sang along with "Purple People Eater." Dad was ready to talk after that.

"If you can't ride, how come you brought all your riding clothes?"

"I did?"

"Unless you've got something other than your high boots that would make all those lumps in your suitcase, I'm pretty sure you did."

I looked at him in astonishment. Had I actually done

that? "It was pure reflex, Dad," I said. "People always remember what's really important to them, so I never forget to bring my riding clothes. I just forget when I can't use them!"

"So, how did you do on items that other people don't forget, like toothbrush, comb, and clean underwear?"

I cast my mind back to the packing process. I could remember putting in my riding clothes. I'd included some summer dresses, shorts, even a bathing suit. Then I re-called the rest of it. "No, no, and yes," I said.

"We'll pick up a toothbrush and comb when we get to the city," he said. "Toothpaste?"

I *am* a flake about everything but horses. "We'd better get some toothpaste, too," I said. "I don't like that stuff you use. It's too good for you."

"If you can't ride, does that mean you can't be around horses?"

I had to think for a second. I'd done what I could to get myself as far from Starlight as possible so I wouldn't be tempted to ride. I wasn't so sure about other horses. Then I remembered that Stevie was planning to spend all her time at Pine Hollow. That was about as close to horses as you could get.

"Nope. I can be around them. I just can't ride them."

"Good," he said. "Because there are two days during this meeting when I'll have to go on a retreat. I wasn't sure what you'd do then, so I called Dorothy DeSoto. She and Nigel are going to be home and would love to have you come out to Long Island to visit them at their stable. Will that be okay?"

Okay wasn't the right word. Fabulous was closer to it.

I LOVE NEW YORK. There's so much happening. I mean it's confusing and all, but there are those millions of people, all of whom seem to know where they are going—and they're in such a hurry to get there! It inspires me to want to know where I'm going, too.

Dad planned to have a couple of days just with me before his conference began. Walking around New York with my father, doing one thing and another, is just as wonderful as riding in a car alone with him. He really is a terrific guy—even if he teases more than he really ought to.

I woke up early our first morning in the city. We were staying in a big hotel with room service, so I ordered this wonderful breakfast for us—fresh fruit, eggs, sausage, orange juice, coffee for Dad, and hot chocolate for me.

Anyway, once we finished eating—and the waiter had come and rolled the breakfast table back out of our suite (isn't that neat?)—we got dressed and headed out to see the world—the world of New York City, that is.

Our first stop was F.A.O. Schwarz. It's one of the biggest toy stores in the world and it's a magical place to be. From the minute you walk in, you feel like you've arrived at Oz or something. There are adorable, wonderful toys everywhere and they put a lot of them out to play with.

"Trains. We're going to see the trains," Dad announced. There was no arguing with that. We went up the escalator and found the train sets. There were a couple of different-size sets, all up and running through worlds of their own with little tracks, trains, stations, trees, and houses. The trains crisscrossed one another, stopping and starting in perfect harmony. Dad could hardly keep his eyes off them. I liked it when they blew their whistles and puffed little O's of smoke.

"Wish you had a son?" I asked, watching him. He was mesmerized by the miniature world.

He put his arm around my shoulder and gave me a little squeeze. "I wouldn't trade you for anything," he assured me. "However, I also wouldn't mind if you'd ask for a train set now and again."

"No way," I said. "I mean it's cute and all, but what's there to play with? All you can do is watch the trains go in circles. Now, if you want me to ask for a toy—and one that's a lot cheaper than a train set—let's talk about horses!"

I had already spotted them, too. The horses weren't far from the train sets and I yanked Dad's hand until he finally relented. Between you and me, I think he already knew I was going to want one, so he was prepared.

There was a wide selection of model horses at the store, but I didn't have any trouble at all making up my mind because the first thing I saw was a model that looked almost exactly like Starlight! He was a big bay with a star on his forehead and he was jumping over a fence.

"That one, please," I said, pointing for the benefit of a saleswoman.

"Good choice," she said. "He's a beauty, isn't he?"

"He looks just like my horse," I explained. "My horse is named Starlight and he's a super jumper and one day he'll be a champion, and so will I, and even though it's just about twenty-four hours since I last saw him, I miss him already because he's the nicest horse in the world although when I got him he wasn't completely trained, but he's just about all trained now because I've been working very hard with him. I ride him almost every day, you know. You really have to do it if you're serious about training and showing your own horse. See—"

I would have gone on, except the saleswoman was talking to Dad.

"My daughter was exactly the same," she said. "Horse-crazy."

"And what's she doing now?" Dad asked. I could tell he was wondering what the future held for me.

"She's an ophthalmologist."

No way. If you're truly horse-crazy, it's for life. I haven't decided what I'm going to be when I grow up, but it's not going to be an ophthalmologist. I'm going to work with horses. I might be a show rider, a breeder, an instructor, or a veterinarian. Preferably all of them. I'm going to be busy in my future!

Dad paid for the horse and handed it to me. The saleswoman waved good-bye and wished me good luck. She wished Dad good luck, too. I think parents of horse-crazy kids don't understand, but that's okay, as long as they keep on letting us be horse-crazy.

"Do you think buying a model horse is the same as riding?" Dad asked. I knew he was teasing a little. He thought the pledge Lisa and I had made for Stevie was a little silly and that was his way of saying it.

"Of course not," I told him. "Stevie's spending the time working with horses. The only thing we can't do is to get on them."

"How about be pulled by them?" Dad asked. He pointed to a whole long line of horse-drawn cabs meant to take people for rides in Central Park.

It was tempting, I've got to admit. The horses weren't any beauties like the ones I'm used to riding. They were good strong draught horses, some not very well groomed at that. Still, there's something wonderful about the scent

132

of a horse and leather and even these dusty old hansom cabs could offer that.

Riding in one of the cabs wouldn't be exactly the same as riding a horse, but I had to say no. I did take a moment to pat a couple of the horses, though, and one of the drivers had a carrot for me to give to his horse, a big old gray gelding with a velvety soft nose. I think he liked me. I gave him a hug and then patted him to say good-bye.

"You're being a very good friend," Dad said.

"Stevie's always been a good friend to me," I reminded him.

"Okay, then if we can't ride, we walk. Come this way."

We went into the park. It's almost odd to call it a park because on a sunny summer day, there were more people there than trees, but that's the way New York is. It was only a short walk to the zoo and the first thing we saw there were the pony cart rides.

"My treat," Dad said.

"Your *tease* you mean. Nope. I'm not going to do it."

He knew I wouldn't anyway. Those carts are teeny and meant for very young children.

"I understand there's a camel ride at the Bronx Zoo. How about that?"

"Da-ad!"

I thought he had the idea then. We went through the rest of the zoo, looking at everything. Some people think zoos are cruel because they keep animals caged up, but that's almost the same thing as saying that it's cruel to keep a horse in a stable and to ride him. As long as the zoo animals are well fed and gently tended, it's all right with me.

"This way, honey," Dad said, tugging my hand when we came out of the last "house" at the zoo. He took me upstairs, past the polar bears. We kept on going uphill, then crossed a road, and by then, I could hear a sound I knew. It was a calliope. We were right by the carousel.

"Dad!" I said, realizing that he'd determined to get me on a horse no matter what. "I can't ride. And that's that."

"Even a carousel? What's going to happen that's so bad if you sit on a wooden horse for five minutes?"

"Veronica diAngelo could join The Saddle Club," I said. "That's what could happen."

"I don't see what Veronica has to do with Stevie's unmentionable wound."

"She's the 'or else' in our deal. If any one of us gets on a horse before Stevie's underside is better, that person has to invite Veronica to join The Saddle Club."

Dad sat down on a nearby bench. It was more than he could take standing up. He knew what a totally horrid person Veronica was and knew that it was unthinkable for her to join The Saddle Club.

"I see," he said. "You aren't just good friends to Stevie, are you? Loyalty and friendship don't begin to describe what's going on here, do they?"

I sat down next to him. "We take it seriously when we

make a pledge to one another, just like you take your promises seriously, Dad."

"I don't know, honey. When I consider what Veronica means to you three—well, I'm not sure I ever took a pledge *that* seriously!"

He was teasing again and that was okay. It meant he understood. That's all I wanted.

"Okay, Carole, now I understand why you *really* don't want to ride. But I've got to say that I don't think there's anybody over the age of about three who would mistake a carousel horse for the real thing."

I looked over at the carousel, spinning gaily, with little children perched on the wooden horses that went up and down as they went around. I knew I'd been acting a little silly. It wasn't the same thing. Stevie and Lisa would surely agree.

"Okay, Dad. I'll go if you'll ride with me."

"I wouldn't miss it for the world," he said.

We rode three times. It was great!

TWO DAYS LATER, I took the train out to the town on Long Island where Dorothy DeSoto has her stable. She trains horses and riders for shows now that she can't ride in them herself. When she got thrown from Topside at the horse show and fractured something in her back, her doctors told her she'd be all right, but she could never ride again. I don't call that being "all right," but I guess it's better than being in a wheelchair, which is where she could end up if she ever hurt that part of her back again.

Dorothy is a great trainer for both horses and riders. This trip I'd have a chance to watch her working with some excellent riders. Dad was worried that it would be temptation for me since I couldn't ride. I wasn't worried about that; Dorothy couldn't ride, either. What it was going to be was pure inspiration. Imagine having the chance to watch one of the finest trainers in the world in action.

Another thing Dad worried about was my getting there. He shouldn't have. It was easy. The train left more or less when it said it would and it got to Dorothy's stop more or less when it said it would and Nigel, Dorothy's husband, was right there waiting for me. He gave me a hug and before he was finished hugging me, he said, "We've got to find a phone!" He made it sound like an emergency so I asked him what was up.

"It's your father."

"Dad? What's the matter?"

"Matter? Nothing. He just wants you to call him the minute you arrive so he can stop worrying."

That was just like Dad and although it was a little annoying, I didn't mind. He's been overprotective of me for some time. It's just a way of showing his love.

"I got here safe and sound," I promised him.

"And was Nigel there to pick you up?" Dad asked.

"Of course he was. That's why I called, Dad. Now you go off on your retreat and do the things you Marines do together and don't worry about me at all. I'm in good hands."

"I know that, honey. I just like to be careful."

"Thanks, Dad. Good-bye."

"Bye."

Nigel was waiting for me outside the phone booth. "Is he okay?" he asked.

"He's okay. He's just always super-cautious. It's because he loves me."

"I could tell," Nigel said. "Dorothy and I love you, too, and we promised your dad we'd take very good care of you. In fact, I'm supposed to stop at the pharmacy and pick up some extra vitamins for you. . . ."

It took a little doing, but I talked Nigel out of the vitamins. I was in too much of a hurry to see Dorothy and her horses to worry about my B-complexes!

"There's no need to hurry to see Dorothy," Nigel said. "She's giving a lesson now and shouldn't be interrupted."

"I wouldn't interrupt. I'd just watch," I said.

"Not with this student. Anything counts as an interruption for her."

"Who is she?" I asked. "Are there some sort of secret training rituals that nobody's supposed to see?"

"Not exactly, but I suppose it's close. She's a fourteen-year-old girl named Beatrice Benner."

There was something about the way Nigel said "Beatrice" that made me know this wasn't any normal fourteen-year-old girl. Ordinarily, I pronounce that name with somewhere between two and three syllables—between Bee-triss and Bee-uh-triss. The way Nigel said it, I swear it had four or five syllables and sounded sort of like this: Bee-aaah-tuh-reeeaaass. It wasn't just because Nigel's English. The look on his face as he uttered that name said worlds.

"Difficult student, huh?"

138

He held his lips tightly together and then mimicked zipping his lips shut. I giggled. That's the sort of thing I love about Nigel. At first, you think he's this proper stuffy English rider and then he'll do something silly like that.

"Ms. Benner is working with a new horse named Southwood. Southwood is pure Thoroughbred. His bloodlines are better than hers—oops, I shouldn't say stuff like that."

"It's okay, Nigel. I'm good at forgetting stuff like that. Go ahead. Talk freely. It's going to be easier on both of us."

"Thanks, Carole. You probably understand this as well as I do. We rely on Dorothy's students, both the horses and the riders, to sustain us. Some of them are difficult. That holds for both the horses and the riders. Dorothy can train manners into the horses, but it's not so easy when it comes to the riders and we're stuck with them because they are her clients and they are the ones who tell their friends how good a trainer Dorothy is."

"I know about that kind of thing, Nigel. After all, Max has been putting up with Veronica diAngelo for a long time just because her father is a very rich and important man in the town and her mother talks a lot to her friends."

"But isn't she a good rider, too?"

I had to stop and think about that for a second. Most of the time, I'll notice the way a person rides long before I notice anything else about them. In Veronica's case, I usually made an exception because she is so obnoxious, but the fact was Nigel was right. Veronica *was* a pretty good rider.

"Not good enough to make up for all the rest of it," I said. That was true, too, as far as I was concerned.

Nigel nodded knowingly. By then I'd spotted the sign for the stable and I knew we were near. Nigel turned into the long drive that curved through the hills of Long Island before coming to a turnaround in front of a big old white house. It wasn't the white house I saw first, though, it was the even bigger stable out back and the paddocks containing a schooling ring, a jump course, and open spaces for some of the horses. One of them was out there right then. He was a sleek dark bay gelding with white stockings on three legs.

As soon as Nigel brought the car to a stop, I jumped right out and ran over to the paddock where the horse was playing and prancing. I held out my hand in greeting. He came right over to me.

"He's a beauty!" I said to Nigel, who stood nearby, watching.

"Meet Southwood," he said. I was only too happy to do so. Nigel said he'd see me in a minute and then turned to carry my backpack into the house. I gave Southwood a cheek rub and then patted his neck. He nodded his head just as if he were trying to tell me how much he liked what I was doing. He wasn't just beautiful; he was smart. I was having such a nice visit with Southwood that I never saw his owner arrive.

"Excuse me!" It was the voice of a young girl. I turned

and saw someone about my own age wearing riding clothes and striding toward me. I guessed it was the infamous Ms. Beatrice Benner and began to introduce myself.

"Hi, I'm—"

"That's my horse," she interrupted.

"I know and he's wonderful!" I said.

"He's *mine*. Please don't touch him."

I couldn't believe my ears, but I withdrew my hand immediately. I recalled what Nigel had said about Southwood and Beatrice being important to Dorothy so I didn't say *any* of the things I wanted to say. I just said, "Sorry."

"Quite all right," Beatrice said to me, as if she were forgiving my unpardonable offense.

"You must be Beatrice Benner," I said. I made as many syllables out of Beatrice as I could, but I had nothing on Nigel. Three was max for me. It was at least nearly enough for her. She smiled, ever so faintly, as if to acknowledge the truth of my statement.

"I'm Carole Hanson," I said. "I'm a friend of Dorothy and Nigel's. I'm staying here for a couple of days."

"How nice for you," Beatrice said. I don't know how she managed it, but the message she conveyed was more like "Aren't you lucky, you underprivileged child, to have the opportunity to stay with people of the caliber of Dorothy and Nigel?" It gave me the shivers. It also made me react strangely. I started sort of blurting out things as if I had to impress her.

"I'm from Virginia," I began. "I study there with Max

Regnery at Pine Hollow Stable in Willow Creek. That's where Dorothy got her early training, you know. We have the same teacher. Max is just wonderful and he's very proud of everything that Dorothy's accomplished. I was at the horse show with my friends when Dorothy had her accident. Now I've been in New York with my father—he's a colonel in the Marine Corps—but I'm staying here while he's on a retreat."

"Oh, you're *that* Carole," Beatrice said. How many Caroles was she expecting?

I gave up. This one was worse than Veronica diAngelo. I would be civil to her because it was important to Dorothy, but I wouldn't spend any more time with her than I absolutely had to, and since I wasn't going to be permitted to touch her horse, there wasn't any reason to stand there.

"I have to see to my luggage," I said. I turned on my heel and walked into the house. *Luggage.* Isn't that good? I gave her the impression that my Louis Vuitton-matched luggage was waiting until the upstairs maid could unpack it for me—instead of the government-issue backpack I'd borrowed from Dad. Over the years, I've learned a couple of things about snobbery from Veronica diAngelo. I thanked her under my breath as I entered the house.

IT TOOK ME a good forty-five seconds to "see to my luggage," and as soon as that was done, I went downstairs to find Nigel. He'd made me a glass of lemonade and suggested that we sit in the living room.

It was a big comfortable living room and the nicest feature of it was a picture window that overlooked the schooling ring. Some people like to see hills or lakes or oceans from their picture windows. I'm always happy looking at a schooling ring.

"Now bring him 'round, Beatrice," Dorothy was saying —barely audible through the glass—"and make him strut his stuff."

I watched. With almost no perceivable signals, Beatrice brought Southwood to a full turn, beautifully executed. It wasn't like the horse's head went first and then the rest followed. His whole body was part of the turning process —just the way it was supposed to be. Then the horse and rider fairly pranced the full length of the school. Everything I'd thought about Southwood turned out to be true. His stride and his deportment were perfect. He responded to the tiniest signals and behaved like the gentleman he was. The part I didn't like to admit was that Bea was a really excellent rider. The horse did what he was supposed to do because he was well trained, but even the best-trained horse can't think for himself. The rider has to know what to ask of the mount. Bea knew.

"I wish she weren't so good," I said, almost unaware that I was speaking.

"Ah, you've met her!" Nigel said. Then he laughed.

So did I. "I think they invented the word obnoxious just for Bea."

"Bea? Is that what you called her?"

"Oh, no, of course not. I never would insult her directly, I promise. I just think of her as 'Bea' because I'm sure she would hate it."

"Exactly," Nigel agreed. "And we'll keep it between us."

"Can't I even tell Dorothy?" I teased.

"Of course you can, but she won't be as amused as you and I are. She has her own stock of names for Ms. Benner and none of them are as flattering as 'Bea.'"

Southwood came pounding past the window then, drawing our attention back to the good side of Beatrice—

her riding skills. Dorothy had set up a hunter jumping course and Beatrice and Southwood were going through the paces perfectly. In this kind of jumping, speed and height aren't really important. What counts is style and Southwood had it. So, I'm sorry to have to report, did Bea. The two of them rode the course at a smooth and even pace, taking the jumps almost as if they weren't there. The horse fairly floated over them, landing without missing a beat. It was a blue-ribbon performance, if I'd ever seen one.

"Takes your breath away, doesn't it?" I asked Nigel.

"Yes, it does. Both Beatrice and her horse are extremely promising. Beatrice has been in a number of shows and done very well, but she's now training with her new horse where she expects to do even better. Southwood is still quite young. He's only just ready for shows so none of the showing he's going to do this year is going to be critical. Dorothy expects that Beatrice and Southwood will grow together and someday—well, who knows?"

When Bea finished the course and was taking a brief rest, Dorothy looked in through the window and waved a greeting to me and Nigel. Then she signaled me to come on out.

"Nah, she's just being polite, isn't she?" I asked Nigel. I wasn't awfully eager to get within twenty yards of Bea again.

"No, I think she actually wants your help. Can you give her a hand?"

"Me? Help?"

Nigel winked at me. "She's not looking for professional pointers, Carole. I think she just needs a hand with something."

Of course, that was just what she had in mind. I went on out into the paddock and gave her a quick hug to return the greeting and to offer to help however she needed me.

"Nice round on the jumps!" I said to Bea, unable to contain my excitement at her skill.

Bea smiled weakly, insincerely. "I'm sure you know what you're talking about," she said.

It was more than Dorothy could take. "Actually, Carole is a very accomplished rider, Beatrice. She was reserve champion at Briarwood." Bea didn't blink. I picked up the cue and continued.

"I ride almost every day," I said. "And when I can't ride, I spend time with my friends and we talk about horses. We call ourselves The Saddle Club."

The minute I said the words, I was sorry. The look on Bea's face told me she thought the club was childish. That's how much *she* knows. I didn't mind her poor opinion. I just wished I'd never invited it.

"Carole's been riding ever since she was a little girl," Dorothy said. "She began riding on Marine Corps bases. You know the Marines have a long history of excellence in horsemanship."

147

"No, I didn't know," she said. She made it sound like she didn't care.

"Carole's father is a colonel in the Marines," Dorothy added. I realized then that she was doing the same thing I'd been doing before, trying to boast about me to make Bea think more of me. It hadn't worked before and wasn't working then.

"Colonel? I met a general once. Isn't that better than a colonel?"

Can you imagine? But she really said it. And I really answered her, too. I said, "It depends on the colonel."

Later Dorothy told me that she thought I should go into the diplomatic corps if I could come up with an answer like that to a snobby question like Bea's, but I don't want to be anywhere near anyone who behaves like that, ever again.

We stopped talking then (not a minute too soon) and Dorothy gave Bea a very difficult task. She took off Southwood's bridle, put him on a lunge line (which I held in the center of the ring), and had him circle at a canter, going over three relatively low jumps. The idea was for her to be able to guide him with her feet alone and to work on her own balance. She had to rise in the saddle as she jumped, but she wasn't allowed to touch Southwood with her hands. I have to give Bea credit. She did it. And I give Southwood credit, too. He took those jumps as well as he had the ones where Bea had control of the reins.

The minute the lesson was over, Bea hopped down out

of the saddle and headed for her mother's car, which was waiting in Dorothy's driveway. Since I was still holding the lunge line, that left me with the opportunity to take Southwood to his stall and groom him. Apparently Beatrice's rule against touching Southwood did not extend to work involved in caring for him. I *was* good enough for that!

It was a pleasure, too. First I walked him around the ring until he was completely cooled down. Then Southwood followed me obediently into the stable and showed me the way to his stall. I unclipped the lunge line and clipped on some lead ropes, cross-tying him where I could do the grooming. Since Dorothy had had all her early training with Max Regnery, it didn't surprise me to find that everything I needed was in a totally logical place. I was busy with a curry comb when Dorothy arrived.

She gave Southwood a welcoming pat and picked up her tools and joined me in the grooming. Like most horses, Southwood enjoyed the process and enjoyed it even more when he was keeping two people busy at once.

I took a deep breath and asked the question that had been on my mind since I'd first met Bea. "How can you stand her?"

"It all has to do with money and reputation," Dorothy explained. "I need the money, of course, but even more important, it's clear she and Southwood are going to go places. If I'm known as her trainer, well, that's good for me and will get me more students."

"Like her?"

"In skill only, I hope. I mean there can't be many more girls like that, can there?"

"I hope not. On the other hand, I hope there are a lot more horses like Southwood."

"He is wonderful and he's a fast learner. Did Nigel say how old he is?"

"No, he didn't, but let me see if I can tell."

You know the old saying about looking a gift horse in the mouth, right? Well the reason you should look a horse in the mouth—gift or otherwise—is to check his teeth and see how old he is. I got Southwood to open up. His adult teeth were barely worn at all. That meant he was very young, but he was old enough to be trained.

"Hmmm. About four?"

"Right on!" Dorothy said. "I can tell Max has been doing his job!"

"And I can tell you've been doing yours," I said. "Southwood is very obedient for a four-year-old."

Dorothy smiled proudly. "Actually, I think he's been doing most of the work himself. He's smart as can be, but both Beatrice and I have worked him very hard. Now, this weekend, he's going to have his first show experience."

"Tell me about it," I said.

"It's a local show, not a rated one, but it's enough that we'll get to see how he performs under pressure. That's important because Beatrice has registered for the Sussex

County Classic later in the summer and his performance there will be important. If we can find out how he reacts to a competition now, we'll be much better prepared for the Sussex. Frankly, I wish she hadn't signed up for the Sussex. That may be too much pressure too soon, but when Beatrice makes up her mind . . ."

Dorothy didn't have to go on. It was clear that Dorothy might be the coach, but Beatrice was always going to be in charge.

"Can I go to the show on Saturday?"

"Of course you can," Dorothy said. "We're counting on your being there. Who else can groom a horse as well as another student of Max Regnery? Will you do the hoof polish?"

"With pleasure," I promised. "And I'll be in the cheering section, too. It may not be all that easy to cheer for Bea, but it'll be a cinch to root for Southwood."

I gave him a hug then. I'm sure he hugged me back by snuggling up to me, but you're going to have to take my word for it.

6

THE FOLLOWING MORNING I was up and into the stable by 6:30. I suppose it sounds awful to be working so early, but sometimes I think the early morning is the best time of day in the stable. There are a zillion chores to be done. All the horses need to be fed and watered. The ones who are going to have early workouts need to be tacked up. Most of them need at least some grooming. One horse was going out to the paddock for a day of freedom and sunshine. Another needed leg wraps. I'm good at leg wraps.

There's a special quality to the early morning that's hard to describe. Some of it has to do with the Eastern sunlight slicing through the dust-filled air. Some of it is the dewy morning smell of hay. Some of it is the way the horses act, just waking up, waiting to be fed and exercised. Some of it is because only people who seriously love horses are at stables at 6:30. There's a nice feeling among us at that hour.

Dorothy and I worked side by side, barely talking because it was so early and there was so much to do.

By 7:30, Bea arrived. She didn't speak to me at all and that suited me fine. I'd fed Southwood and given him a brushing before I tacked him up for her. I led him out to the schooling ring and wordlessly handed Bea the reins. Wordlessly, she accepted them. I had the funny feeling she'd missed her early childhood lesson on "magic words." It was okay. If she didn't say thank you, I didn't have to tell her she was welcome.

While I held Southwood's head, she mounted him. Southwood was tall, but not so tall that she should have had to pull herself up the way she did. It was a little thing, but I noticed it and it concerned me and as the day wore on, my concern grew.

She and Dorothy had already decided they wouldn't work Southwood too hard since the show was only two days away and he shouldn't be exhausted from the lesson when he was in a competition. Dorothy stood in the middle of the ring.

"Circle at a sitting trot."

Southwood trotted around the ring, but Bea was posting.

"*Sitting!*" Dorothy said.

153

Bea blew her nose. "What?" she asked, the annoyance apparent in her tone of voice.

"Sitting trot," Dorothy said clearly.

Bea sat. Then when Dorothy gave the order to canter, Bea was coughing and couldn't hear her. Dorothy had to say it again.

I could just see this happening in the ring on Saturday. When Bea was good, she was *really* good. That morning, she was not really good. She was bad. It was as if she couldn't pay attention.

She wiped her nose with a tissue again and stuffed it in her pocket. Then she pushed her hard hat back a little and swept her arm across her forehead. All the motion and commotion in the saddle confused poor Southwood, who broke into a trot when he was supposed to be cantering. Bea hit him with her crop. That didn't seem fair to me since I didn't think it had been his fault in the first place, but it did make him try all the harder to please her.

I leaned against the fence of the schooling ring, silently watching Bea have a dreadful lesson. I realized that a lot of good riders have bad days, including me. Maybe it was the pressure of the show only two days away, but I didn't think so. I thought there was something else and the more I watched her, the more sure I was. She coughed, sniffled, and wiped for a full hour. I thought she was sick and didn't want to admit it.

After an hour, Dorothy suggested a fifteen-minute break. Bea rode Southwood right over to me so I could hold his head while she dismounted. That was when I got a close look at her. She was as pale as a ghost. I also noticed some bumps around her neck. They were like little teeny blisters.

"Beatrice, are you all right?" I asked, forgetting for a moment that I wasn't worthy of her attention.

"Of course I'm all right," she snapped.

"But those bumps—" I touched my neck to indicate where I'd noticed them.

Her hand went to her neck reflexively, and the second she felt the bump, she glared at me and then at Dorothy.

"Flea bites!" she said disgustedly. "You people can't keep the stable free of pests for animals *or* people."

You people? It occurred to me to wonder who she had in mind, but her attitude was so rotten that I didn't really care. It's true that horses do sometimes attract pests that can annoy people as well, but I'd never seen a flea bite that looked like what was on her neck.

By nine o'clock, Bea had had it. I was pretty sure she was too sick to continue; she mumbled something outrageous about having to rid herself of pests and announced that she was going home, presumably to take a bath in DDT. At that point, I didn't care what she did as long as she didn't do it here. I was glad to see her go. If Dorothy shared my enthusiasm, she didn't tell me.

"Too bad. If a rider has a bad lesson before a show, she's more likely to lack confidence in the competition."

"Bea, lack confidence? I don't think that's her problem, Dorothy. I wouldn't worry about that one."

"I guess I'm overreacting, huh? Well, Southwood still needs his exercise. Want to ride him?"

I did, of course. I wanted to ride him about as much as I've ever wanted anything in my whole life (except for owning Starlight, I'd wanted that more), but I couldn't do it and I told Dorothy so.

"What do you mean you can't ride?"

"It has to do with The Saddle Club. We made a promise to one another."

"To not ride?" Her surprise was to be expected. After all, it did sound kind of weird.

"It has to do with Stevie, see."

Dorothy grinned. "I suspected as much. Everything truly strange about The Saddle Club has to do with her."

"And everything really wacky fun, too, remember."

"I remember, so what's the story this time?"

I told her about Stevie's underside problem and the pledge we'd made.

"You know, I haven't ridden a horse, other than at a *very* stately walk, since my accident. I miss it more than I can possibly tell you. I can't imagine choosing to be grounded. That's a real act of friendship and loyalty on your part."

I knew Dorothy would understand.

"But just because you can't ride doesn't mean you can't

156

work. So, take Southwood on a lead and run him around the ring a couple of times and then walk him until he's cooled down. Then we'll have lunch and after that, we'll give his show grooming a trial run. Deal?"

"Deal."

THE NEXT MORNING, I was up again at six and down in the stable by 6:30. I suppose it was sort of a trial run for me. How was I going to like the life of a trainer when I grew up, if it meant getting up at very early hours? I knew the answer: just fine!

I began working on Southwood right away because I wanted him perfectly groomed by the time Bea arrived. I did a good job, too. His coat was gleaming when Dorothy came into the stable at 7:00. By 7:30 when Bea was to arrive, his hooves were clean as could be and coal black with hoof polish. He was ready.

Unfortunately, Bea wasn't. The phone rang at 7:30 and it was Bea's mother. Bea was too sick to make the call herself. She had chicken pox.

Now, don't get me wrong. I never wished illness on

anybody—at least not serious illness—and even though I didn't like Beatrice one bit, I hadn't been involved in her getting sick. She'd gotten chicken pox all by herself. Her mother told Dorothy that Beatrice was just miserable, itching, scratching, and sore. I can't swear to you that it broke my heart.

It meant, first of all, that I could spend the entire day around Southwood without any fear of someone telling me to remove my hands from *her* horse.

I turned to Dorothy. "You know Southwood is going to need a lot of exercise to keep limber for the show tomorrow, so I think I'll work him on a lunge line. He almost doesn't need a rider anyway, so it'll be perfect!"

"That's where you're wrong," Dorothy said.

"I am?"

"He does need a rider. He's got to be in the show tomorrow. It's really important for him to have the experience. It's not that it's an important show, but we want him to become familiar with the world of shows so that when he's in an important one, he won't freak out. You know the way some horses are the first time they're away from home. They balk at the van, they balk at the temporary stalls, they balk at all the new horses they've never seen before, and they behave terribly in the ring. Southwood may have to get that stuff out of his system and I'd much rather have him do it at the local show tomorrow than the Sussex County Classic."

It made sense to me. "So is Bea going to be ready to ride tomorrow?"

"Not if she's itching and scratching, and besides, I think she's still very contagious. Speaking of which, you've had chicken pox, haven't you?"

"When I was three. I'm glad I don't remember any of it."

"Then at least we can be pretty sure you'll be healthy tomorrow."

"Of course I will. I wouldn't miss the show for anything. I can't wait to watch Southwood perform."

"I wasn't thinking in terms of watching," Dorothy said. Then she gave me a meaningful look.

I got a funny feeling about it. "What are you talking about?"

"I want you to ride Southwood tomorrow."

"Me?"

"Is there another old girl standing here with me who would qualify to ride in the junior events?"

"On Southwood?"

"Yes."

I've got to tell you that the first thing that entered my mind was utter joy. I was thrilled at the very idea of being able to ride this magnificent animal, especially in a competition. I knew he didn't have much chance of doing well, what with a new rider in a new circumstance, but just the thought of it gave me the nicest chills.

"Of course!" And then it came to me. "But I can't. I'm sorry. I can't."

"You what?"

"Stevie—our pledge. Remember? I can't ride until she's better."

"Maybe we could call her and see how she's doing?"

I knew how she was doing. She still had a very sore sitting place. No way.

"If you asked her, she'd say yes."

"Maybe, but maybe she'd say no and it wouldn't be fair. We made a pledge to one another. We take it seriously. You should, too."

"I do, I really do," Dorothy said and I knew she meant it. Some grown-ups might have made fun of the promise The Saddle Club had made, but Dorothy knew that we meant the things we'd said and she genuinely respected it. "Come on," she said. "Let's go to the house, have some breakfast, and see if we can solve this thing."

I fastened the latches on Southwood's stall and followed Dorothy to the kitchen. Dorothy made scrambled eggs with the same confident manner that she trained a horse. In just a few minutes bacon was sizzling in the microwave, eggs were cooking in a frying pan, and I was setting the table.

Nigel joined us just as I poured three glasses of orange juice.

"Why's everyone so quiet?" he asked.

161

"We have a problem," Dorothy said. Then she explained about Bea's chicken pox.

"But, of course, Carole can fill in for her, can't she?" Nigel asked.

"That's the problem," I said. And I explained to him about The Saddle Club pledge. Like Dorothy, he understood that it was a serious pledge.

We sat down to eat and there was no conversation for a while. Then Dorothy spoke.

"Carole, I'm going to ask you to break the pledge and I'm not doing it lightly. I'm not doing it for me. I'm not even doing it for Beatrice, and I don't expect you would do it for either of us. I'm doing it for Southwood. He needs to be in the show. He's entered there. He needs a junior rider. You're a junior rider and you're qualified for the show. I only need to ask the judges to accept you as a substitute for Beatrice. They'll understand and accept, I'm sure. I can't ride for Beatrice and neither can Nigel. I don't have another student who could fill in. All my other riders are adults. That leaves you. If you say no, I'll understand, but if you say yes, Southwood will be the one who benefits most."

I'd like to tell you I had to think about it long and hard, but it wouldn't be true. When Dorothy explained it in terms of how important it was for Southwood, I couldn't say no. I had to do it and ignore the possible consequences. Well, not ignore them, exactly.

"You can't tell anyone at Pine Hollow. Lisa and Stevie can *never* know."

"They won't hear it from me," Dorothy pledged.

"Me, neither," Nigel added.

"Don't worry," Dorothy said. "There won't be anything to tell. It's Southwood's first show. He's sure to blow it. You won't win anything, but I will because I'll learn a lot about Southwood from watching his public debut."

Somehow it seemed okay that I was doing it for Southwood. Way back in the recesses of my mind was a secret little smile for the fact that Bea would know *I'd* been the one to ride her horse in his first show. That was the part of me that hoped I'd win a blue ribbon. The rest of me knew that a ribbon was the least of my worries.

"Thank you, Carole," Dorothy said. "Now, what are we going to find to put on you to wear in the show?"

"I brought all my riding clothes," I told her.

"Even though you knew you wouldn't ride?"

"Some things are just automatic," I confessed.

Dorothy laughed. "I do exactly the same thing with my horse clothes and then I always forget my toothbrush! Did you remember yours?"

"I sure did. I mean, I remembered the toothbrush Dad bought for me in New York, since of course I forgot my own at home."

"Birds of a feather . . ." Nigel said, watching the two of us.

"You should talk!" Dorothy said. "Remember the time

163

you didn't bring any street shoes for a weekend in Chicago?"

"And I had three pairs of riding boots with me, didn't I? Guilty as charged!"

We finished breakfast much more cheerfully than we'd begun it. Then while Dorothy and Nigel put the dishes in the dishwasher, I skipped up to my room and slipped into my riding clothes. It felt wonderful to be back in them.

8

SATURDAY MORNING, I was too busy with the things I had to do to be worried about the things I was going to do. My mind was a blur of dos and don'ts, didn'ts, wouldn'ts, and couldn'ts.

I'd spent three hours on Southwood on Friday—as much time as Dorothy thought he ought to be exercised, but I didn't think it had been anywhere near enough for me. Once we put Southwood back in his stall, Dorothy and I just talked and talked about techniques and goals.

My main goal for the day was to be with Southwood and see how he reacted to everything at the show. Dorothy would see most of it, but, as a rider, there would be things I learned that she didn't.

"He's going to be nervous, but he's a smart horse," she said. "If you feel he knows what he's doing, let him do it the way he wants to do it. It's okay if he makes a couple of mistakes. I can learn from them and share my learning with Beatrice."

So the most important thing I had to remember was to let Southwood be Southwood. It was as if Dorothy wanted to see him at his worst so she knew what to protect against the next time.

It quickly became apparent that Southwood didn't have a "worst" side. He stepped onto the van like a pro. He stepped off it like an old hand. I led him to his temporary stall. He took a minute or two to see what other horses were around him and then he took a bite of hay. It was as if he were saying, "All right, so I'm here, so what's the fuss?"

I wish I could have been as calm as he was. My own stomach wasn't filled with hay, but butterflies! I haven't had much show experience. Max is more concerned with us competing against ourselves, trying to be the best we can, than with having us compete against others. It doesn't mean he's against showing—not at all. It's just that he feels that we each should have our own goals at a show and if we meet those goals, we've really earned a blue ribbon, no matter how well we've done compared to other riders.

I agree with that philosophy; I've learned a lot from it, too. Still, there's another dimension to a show and that is that it gives riders a chance to see how they measure up to others by certain standards.

In other words, I wanted to win.

Southwood and I were entered in only one event and that was the hunter jumper class. Because of the peculiar circumstances of me filling in for Bea, I had to go through some formalities, such as meeting the judges and making a personal petition for the substitution. Mostly, they just wanted to know that I wasn't some sort of hustler pretending to be an intermediate rider. Dorothy vouched for me on that score. I thought my own skill in the saddle would speak for me, too.

Once that was done, successfully, I had only a little over an hour to get Southwood ready. Dorothy and I groomed him to within an inch of perfection. Then I put on my own breeches and boots, added a blouse and jacket of Dorothy's, and I was ready to meet the world, alone, except for Southwood and forty thousand butterflies in my stomach.

"You're going to do splendidly," Dorothy assured me. I loved it when she used words like "splendidly." Nigel, of course, said things like "splendidly" a lot. Of course I'd heard him say "awesome," too, so I suppose he was being Americanized at the same time Dorothy was being Anglicized!

I'd drawn the eighth starting place for the event. That was eighth out of fifteen. There are a lot of theories about order in a competition. Some people say you should be first and set the standard nobody else can meet. Others say, be last so you know what you have to beat. I was smack in the middle. I expected to disappear into the background and that was what Dorothy expected, too. Eighth start was just fine under the circumstances— "splendid," in fact.

There was a wide range of talent among the junior riders in the class. Some of the kids (ten girls, five boys) had been riding a good long time. There were a couple I thought were really good.

"Look at the way that girl is taking the jumps!" I said to Dorothy as a girl named Emilie seemed to soar through the course.

"Not bad, but she's rushing. If she learns patience, she'll be a good rider. Someday."

I watched more carefully, trying to learn.

Then there was a boy named Francis. He was quite young and it seemed to be his first show. He was fidgeting nervously with his hands.

"Boy, he's going to blow it," I remarked, feeling bad for him.

"Just watch," said Dorothy.

The minute Francis and his horse began their performance, it became clear that the horse had all the experience Francis lacked. He went over each jump smoothly and evenly. By the third jump, Francis had stopped fidgeting and they ended up doing very well.

"That's the thing about an experienced horse," Dorothy explained. "The very best of them can make up for a lot of rider flaws. The judges will notice the fidgeting and mark him down, but it's almost as if the horse gets extra credit for being so good!"

By then, there were just three riders until it was my turn on Southwood. I went to mount up and walk in circles for a few minutes until we were called. I wasn't at all sure that walking in circles was going to calm Southwood or warm him up, but I hoped it would keep me from being fidgety like Francis.

The minute I settled into Southwood's saddle, I felt at home. I'd been there for three hours the day before, and it seemed like we were old friends who'd never been separated at all.

I gave him the slightest signals with my legs and he responded obediently and gracefully. This horse had a style that's hard to come by. He really wanted to please me and as far as I was concerned, he was doing a fine job of it.

I was totally prepared for him to balk. I expected him to shy at some of the strange horses. I expected him to fidget while we waited our turn. I expected him to stomp nervously, perhaps to bolt into the ring when I signaled him to start. I thought he might be turned around and confused by the audience or flustered by the unfamiliar surroundings. He let me down completely on every one of these expectations. He performed as if he'd been in a show ring from the moment of his birth. Nothing upset him in the least.

I'd studied the course of the jumps and had a good idea

of how I wanted to approach them. I knew that style was all for this class. What I didn't know was how much style Southwood had!

He fairly pranced into the ring and then as I got him set for the first jump, he seemed to collect himself so he could concentrate on the job at hand. He broke into an effortless, silky-smooth canter. I know that's a funny way to describe the gait that most people compare to a rocking horse, but that's the way it was with Southwood. As we approached each jump, I had enough time to decide exactly where I wanted to be when we took off and then when I gave him the signal, we did it. Some people describe a jump as soaring or flying. On Southwood, it was more like floating. Again, I was completely unaware of any work on his part; he just did it.

The course snaked back and forth, calling for a number of sharp turns at either end of the rectangular ring. Southwood brought his entire body into a turn just the way the very best dressage horses manage to do it. He never lost a step or a beat; he never slowed down or speeded up. He maintained the exact pace I'd set for him. He jumped like an angel.

I quickly remembered Francis on his horse who made him look good. I knew I was a better rider than Francis, but even at that, Southwood was making *me* look good.

At some point during the jump course, I completely ceased being aware of the audience, the judges, even Dorothy and Nigel. It was as if the whole world were simply

170

Southwood and me and we were not two, but one and that was enough.

At Southwood's landing over the last jump, the whole audience burst into applause. Since the audience primarily consisted of the parents and grandparents of the other kids in the competition, I knew we'd done something very special.

"Oh, Carole!" Dorothy greeted me. The grin on her face told me she was proud of me. She didn't have to say the rest, but she did. "You were *wonderful!*"

"Not me. Southwood. I don't know about Bea being a champion, but this fellow's a champion through and through. He made his rider look good today and he'll make his trainer look good for many years to come. You picked a winner, Dorothy. I just sat there and let him do it all."

"And he did it, didn't he?"

"He sure did!"

I stood up in the stirrups, swung my right leg back over the saddle, and let myself slide to the ground. Then I gave Southwood about one-sixteenth of the hug he deserved.

I didn't pay too much attention to any of the rest of the riders. Some were better than others. Two of them were disqualified because their horses refused to jump. Another had a problem because she took the jumps in the wrong order. One of the girls' horses bucked a few times and that's not good form. Mostly I was thinking that I had done what I'd come for and I was ready to go home. In fact, I started to untack Southwood.

"Hold it, there, Carole," Dorothy said, refastening the buckle I'd undone.

"Shouldn't we go home now?" I asked.

"It's generally considered a good idea to wait until the ribbons are announced," Dorothy said.

I don't know why, but I was surprised by that. I had wanted to win, but my goal really wasn't to get a ribbon. I was only there because Southwood needed the experience and by riding in the show, Dorothy had learned that he was really good. What none of us had been prepared for was exactly how good he was.

This being a junior class, the judges like to give a lot of ribbons. Not everyone can win and all the competitors know that, but when Dorothy said they had eight ribbons to award, I realized I might get one. Still, I wasn't prepared for receiving first prize. That was a blue ribbon and a very large round of applause. I gaped at Dorothy when they announced my number.

"Didn't you know?" she said.

"Uh-uh."

"Well, I did. So go get your prize, you goose," she said, giving Southwood an encouraging pat on his rump.

He loved it. If he'd been happy about being in the ring for a performance, he positively preened when we returned to garner the rewards of our labors! All the other ribbon winners were waiting patiently. The judges greeted us warmly and then clipped the ribbon on Southwood's bridle.

"Would you like to lead the victory gallop?" the judge asked me.

I'd forgotten about that. Southwood and I were only too happy to oblige. We circled the entire ring at a gallop and then were joined for a second go-round by all the other riders while all the proud parents and grandparents applauded like crazy. Nobody applauded louder than Dorothy, though. I was very happy for her.

I was happy for myself, too. Even though this wasn't a big show, I'd had an opportunity to do well and it had worked out well. I'd had an almost magical ride on an exceptional horse and I'd gotten a blue ribbon that would make Beatrice Benner so jealous she wouldn't be able to see straight.

That was the good news, of course. I'd certainly one-upped Beatrice. She would probably *say* it was just because Southwood was an outstanding horse, but the ribbon was *mine* not hers, and somewhere in her mind, she would always have to wonder if she would have gotten the blue herself. I gloated on that one. I admit it.

In fact I was so busy gloating that for a while it distracted me from the bad news about Southwood's being such a great show horse. The blue ribbon was mine to keep. But I couldn't ever show it to the people who'd care the most—Stevie and Lisa. I'd broken my promise to my two best friends and my punishment was that I would have to keep this secret forever.

That's a horrible punishment, particularly when it also meant I was going to have to lie to my friends. As much as I dreaded that, it was better than having Veronica di-Angelo in The Saddle Club.

PART IV

Reunion

THE FIRST THING Carole saw when she climbed out of her father's station wagon at Pine Hollow was Stevie Lake in a saddle on Topside.

"Stevie!" she shrieked in joy, running over to her dear friend. "You're better!" Her heart glowed with happiness.

Carole scrambled up the fence that circled the outdoor ring and when she could reach her, she gave Stevie a hug.

"Are you *all* better?" Carole asked.

"Let's just say I'm better enough," Stevie answered. "I'm going to avoid a sitting trot for a few weeks yet, though, but I'm back in the saddle—with my doctor's approval. And I don't have to lug that awful pillow around anymore."

"How wonderful!" Carole's happiness was totally sincere. It was both for Stevie *and* for her.

"That's almost exactly what Lisa said when she arrived here five minutes ago."

"You mean she's already tacking up?"

"Sure. Don't you want to go do that? I asked Max if we could take a trail ride and he said it would be okay. I think he knows that we have a lot to talk about and he figures if he says we have to stay and go to class this morning, we're just going to talk all the way through it and drive him mad."

"That sounds more like Stevie than like Max," Carole commented.

"Well, he did need a little convincing."

"And you were just the person to do it for him, weren't you?"

Stevie smiled proudly. She knew there was nobody in the world better than she at talking Max into things—unless it was Max himself. Stevie remembered his wonderful mistake at the horrible error she'd made with the young kids. She gulped. She had to forget that episode, permanently, now that her friends were home. It wasn't going to be easy, but it was important. She patted Topside and began walking him around the ring slowly to warm him up while she waited for her friends. It did feel awfully good to be back in the saddle—legally.

Carole practically flew into the stable. Starlight was there, almost as if he'd been waiting for her. He greeted her warmly, especially when she gave him two carrots and a sugar lump.

"I don't usually spoil you with sugar, you little sweet tooth, but I missed you so much I can't even tell you!"

She was amused by her own words and then she felt an uncomfortable pang of guilt. There were things she couldn't tell Starlight, just like there were things she couldn't tell Stevie and Lisa. Starlight wouldn't really understand about Southwood. Stevie and Lisa definitely wouldn't understand. A promise was a promise and that blue ribbon was a secret. She hadn't even wanted to tell her father because he and Stevie were such good friends that he might make a mistake and blurt out something about the ribbon to Stevie one day. Dorothy had let the cat out of the bag when he'd arrived the next morning to pick her up and take her back to New York for the rest of their trip. Carole was glad about that, actually. It was a wonderful secret and she was relieved to be able to share it with someone. Now she *might* tell Starlight because she was quite confident he wouldn't tell anybody else, but that was it. Nobody else would ever know.

It took her only a few minutes to tack him up and take him by the good-luck horseshoe, where they ran into Lisa and Stevie.

"Isn't it wonderful?" Lisa asked excitedly as she climbed into Barq's saddle and brushed the horseshoe herself. "I've missed this terribly!"

"Even when you were far from Pine Hollow?" Stevie asked, touching the horseshoe for herself. One of Pine Hollow's many traditions was that all riders were supposed to touch the horseshoe before embarking on a ride. No one who had ever done it had been seriously hurt. The riders were never quite sure whether it was the magical power of the horseshoe or the fact that just touching it reminded them to ride carefully.

Lisa felt a little uncomfortable answering Stevie's question because she had a secret about being on a horse that she couldn't share with Stevie and Carole. Still, she'd made up her mind that she wasn't going to be completely truthful, so she might as well get on with it now.

"Of course we missed riding when we were away from Pine Hollow," Lisa said. "It was probably harder for you because you were here, around all this gorgeous temptation, but don't forget you *couldn't* ride. It would have hurt too much. Carole and I *could* ride. We just didn't." Lisa looked at her friends nervously, afraid they might be able to tell, just by looking at her. Neither seemed to notice anything.

"Well, welcome home!" said a familiar, unwelcoming voice. It was Veronica diAngelo. She was on her Arabian mare, Garnet, ready to go to class. "And Stevie! You're riding again. All better?"

Stevie smiled sweetly. "Yes, Veronica. I am riding again."

"It must have been hard on you to watch your friends ride without you while you were recuperating."

"Where have you been, Veronica?" Stevie asked.

"Paris," she answered simply.

"Well, if you'd been around, you would have known that my friends are very good friends and they felt so bad about the fact that I couldn't ride that they decided not to ride, either, until I could ride again."

"Oh," Veronica said. It was all the comment she was going to make. She reached across the threesome, barely coming in contact with the horseshoe and without another word directed her horse toward the flat class Max was conducting in the outdoor ring.

"I hope she didn't touch the horseshoe and she breaks her neck in class," Stevie sneered.

Lisa and Carole were thinking something along the same lines, but were too polite to say it.

"Let's go," said Lisa. "I can't wait to get my toes into good old Willow Creek!"

Stevie reached over and used her riding crop to unlatch the gate that opened onto the fields. It was a neat way to open the gate, but it didn't work well for closing it. She was going to have to dismount and do it by hand. Before she was out of the saddle, though, Mrs. Reg appeared and did the job for her. The girls thanked her.

"You're very welcome and I'm glad to have you back here. Isn't it great that Stevie's riding again?" They all agreed on that. Then Mrs. Reg turned to Lisa. "Lisa, I hope you had a wonderful time in Los Angeles. Was it great? Did you see that nice young man—what's his name?"

"Skye Ransom. I sure did. He wanted to say hello to everyone here—including you."

"Well, good. And Carole, I *know* you had a good time up there in New York because I read all about you at that horse show. What was the horse's name?"

Carole's heart dropped about six feet. It hadn't occurred to her that there would have been anything written and published about the horse show.

"Horse show?" she said, stalling for time.

"Yes. Wasn't it a hunter class?"

"Hunter class?" Carole knew she was sounding stupid, but it was better than revealing the truth. "This is news to me."

"I'm sure it said 'C. Hanson.' Maybe there's another C. Hanson who's been training with Dorothy DeSoto?"

Carole gulped. It was a stretch, but maybe she could get away with it. "Must be the case. Funny she didn't mention it to me when I saw her."

"Yes, funny," said Mrs. Reg.

Carole put on her brightest smile and turned to her friends. "Shall we head for the woods?"

"I guess so," said Stevie. There was a tone to her voice that struck Carole as odd. It had to be a reaction to the very strange conversation Stevie had just overheard.

THE GIRLS BEGAN at a walk and soon picked up a trot. It had been a very long time since they'd had a chance to ride together and Carole felt that no matter what secret might be hanging over her head, nothing was going to take away from her enjoyment of this day in the field and forest by Pine Hollow.

The rich spicy scent of pine struck Stevie's nose as soon as she and her friends entered the forest. She hadn't been in the woods since the day . . . She didn't even want to think about it. To think about it was to come too close to nearly revealing and she couldn't do that. No way.

"Let's canter!" Lisa called from behind. That seemed a very good way to shake the cobwebs of guilt. Stevie signaled Topside to canter and the three of them followed the flat open trail that led to the creek.

In a matter of minutes, the girls slowed their horses to a walk. They'd reached the quarry. Stevie shivered, remembering how frightened she'd been the last time she'd ridden here and how her worst nightmares had come true, but how it had come out all right. Incredible and, worst of all, untellable. This wasn't fun.

"I'm not sure we should be here, you know," Lisa said, drawing Barq to a stop.

"Why not?" Carole asked, stopping and looking back.

Stevie looked around. "I heard one of the kids say something about a coyote being spotted near the quarry."

"That was just a rumor," Stevie said. "Max had Red check it out and he didn't see anything. I didn't see anything, either. No sign at all."

"You?" Carole asked. "This is a very long walk from Pine Hollow."

Stevie gulped. There was no accusation in Carole's voice, but it was a pointed remark.

"When were you here?" Lisa asked.

"I wasn't here," Stevie said. "It's too far to walk. I never came during the summer. I just mean the whole time I was hanging around Pine Hollow there weren't any signs of coyotes. Nobody said anything about seeing one anywhere in the woods—here by the quarry or anywhere else. I'm sure it's perfectly safe for us, Lisa."

"Oh," Lisa said. "Well, I'm relieved to hear that."

"We should get going," said Stevie. "Topside is just dying for a drink from the creek."

"Okay," Lisa agreed. They continued their journey.

The rest of the trail to the creek was very hilly. There were points where the trees opened up and Lisa enjoyed looking across the rolling Virginia countryside. It was pretty, all right, but it wasn't as dramatic as the ride she and Skye had taken through the mountains in California where they could see the Pacific Ocean and the rough countryside that nature alternately pummeled with wildfires and mud slides. Virginia was nice, but it wasn't California. And she couldn't say a word to her friends. She'd been tempted; she genuinely had been. But one minute with the totally despicable Veronica diAngelo by the good-luck horseshoe demonstrated beyond the shadow of a doubt that the price wouldn't be worth paying. She couldn't tell. She never would. It would be her secret forever and ever.

With every step of Barq's hooves, Lisa's heart became heavier. She thought she was prepared to keep a secret from her friends, but she wasn't prepared to handle the awful guilt she felt about doing it. It was like one gigantic dark cloud and it was going to follow her for the rest of her life.

The more she thought about it, the more unbearable it became. It was one thing to make a rational decision about keeping the secret to herself when she was in Los Angeles and her friends were thousands of miles away. Lisa found that it was another thing altogether when they were all right next to one another.

They neared the creek, dismounted, secured their horses to tree limbs, and within minutes each had her boots and socks off and they were dangling their feet in the deliciously cold water.

It seemed to cleanse more than Lisa's feet. It cleansed her darkened heart, too. Whatever the price, she knew that the one thing in life she could not bear would be lying to her friends. She'd made a promise; she'd broken it. They had to know.

"I have to tell you something," she said finally. When Stevie and Carole looked at Lisa, they both saw their friend's eyes welling up with tears.

"What's the matter, Lisa? Is everyone okay?" Stevie asked, deeply concerned.

Carole's face was filled with sympathy.

"Not really," Lisa said, now totally miserable. She was about to admit something awful to her friends and they were being nice to her. She was sure they'd never be nice to her again.

She had to do it, though. She took a deep breath and then she blurted it all out.

"I lied to you! I did ride. I didn't want to, but Skye invited me and I couldn't resist. I had to do it for Skye. If it had just been me, I would have said no. I mean it. So we went and it was wonderful—just wonderful. I really enjoyed it, but I feel horrible about it and I can't keep it a secret from you!"

Then in came a full blast of tears, inconsolable, unstoppable. When Lisa cried, she really cried.

"I don't believe it!" Carole said.

"I'm only human!" Lisa protested.

"It's not that," Carole said. She tried to give Lisa a hug to comfort her.

"So what is it?" Stevie asked, picking up on something in the tone of Carole's voice.

"I thought I was the only one."

"Only what?" asked Stevie, now fully suspicious.

"Who'd been on a horse, of course."

"You were?" Lisa's tears stopped as suddenly as they'd begun.

"Like Mrs. Reg said. It was a horse show. Dorothy practically begged me."

"And you got a ribbon?" Lisa asked.

"Blue," Carole said. "But I didn't want to do it, Stevie. I promise I tried not to, but it was for the sake of the horse!"

"For the sake of the horse? I did it for the sake of the kids!"

"You did what?" Lisa asked.

"Ride, of course. They'd ridden out by the quarry all alone, see, and I knew they'd be in trouble."

"You rode?" Carole asked. "How'd you manage it with your backside problem?"

"I rode standing the whole way."

187

"Why didn't we think of that in the first place?" asked Lisa.

"Because it only worked so-so and my bottom was even sorer for a week than it had been before. But I had no choice, really. I thought the kids could be in real danger —and they were."

"So what happened" Carole asked.

And Stevie told them. She told them everything about the young kids and how much fun she'd been having with them, and the story of Merlin and the witch of Garrett Road.

"I never heard that one," said Carole.

"I just made it up, Carole," Stevie said. "And I don't think I'll make up any more tall tales again, ever."

"Oh, don't say that, Stevie, you're the best at it!"

"All right, I'll tell tall tales, but everybody is going to have to sign something before I start saying they understand it's a tall tale and isn't true."

"Trust a lawyer's daughter to come up with that," Carole said.

"Two lawyers," Stevie reminded her. Then she went on to finish the story with her favorite part—what Max never knew.

Carole and Lisa had to admit that it was a great story.

"Is it a tall tale?" Lisa asked suspiciously.

"Nope, every sorry word of it is true. Worst of all, I broke the pledge. But since I wasn't alone, I want to hear what happened to each of you."

Lisa went next. Carole and Stevie both liked Skye every bit as much as Lisa did and they understood completely why Lisa couldn't say no. Stevie, who really had a crush on Chris Oliver, made Lisa explain a few times just how obnoxious he was to Skye before she'd believe it.

"Oh, all right," Stevie conceded finally. "So he's a rotten person, but that doesn't mean I can't have a crush on the characters he plays, does it?"

"Only if your friend Phil doesn't mind," Carole teased.

"Phil has a crush on Mindy Manfred—you know, that gorgeous model? That doesn't seem to interfere with our relationship, either."

The girls laughed about that. They decided that fantasy crushes were okay—even when they were on people you'd never meet or know and wouldn't like if you ever did.

Lisa went on. "But even when I knew I couldn't keep Kip and when I got Skye to charter the ambulance plane for Aunt Alison and all of that was the right thing to do, I still felt bad about you two. I just can't lie to you. I mean, I *can*, but it hurts too much."

"Did you turn down Kip because of us?" Stevie asked.

"No. Really, I didn't. I turned him down because I wasn't sure my parents could really afford a horse right now, and because it was too much of a gift for Skye to give me. Even though he's got lots of money, it isn't right."

"We're going to have to talk," Stevie said, putting her

arm around Lisa's shoulder. But she was just teasing and Lisa knew it. Her decision had been the right one.

Then both Stevie and Lisa looked at Carole. It was her turn.

"Well," she began. "There's this girl named Bea. No, actually, her name is Beatrice Benner and she's somebody who makes Veronica diAngelo look like a nice girl next door."

Carole told the whole story—from the first time she touched Southwood and was told to take her hands off the horse to the victory gallop at the horse show.

Then she began whispering. "He really was a magnificent horse to ride—so easy!"

Her friends leaned forward to listen.

"Why are you whispering?" Stevie asked.

"So Starlight won't hear, silly," Lisa explained for Carole, who nodded.

Stevie giggled. "Right," she said. "I get it."

When Carole finished telling her story, the girls were quiet, each feeling her own special form of relief and pleasure at having been able to talk about an adventure she'd had while away from the others.

Lisa sighed. Carole and Stevie followed suit. It was a good time, but there was trouble ahead and each of them knew it.

Lisa spoke first.

"We made a promise, you know. A pledge to one another."

"Yeah," said Stevie.

"And I broke it."

"So did I."

"Me, too."

"We could just forget it," said Stevie. "Couldn't we? I mean if we *all* broke it."

"Then the next pledge we make to one another won't mean anything," Lisa said. "If you don't keep pledges and promises, it means you don't respect the people you made them to."

"What if I just don't respect you-know-who?" She couldn't bring herself to say Veronica's name.

"Stevie!" Carole said.

"I know. I know. I was just trying to make it all go away. But what do we do?"

"We invite Veronica to join The Saddle Club," Carole said. "We have to."

"And then can we immediately disband the club and start all over again under an assumed name? Without her, of course." Stevie asked.

"Stevie!" Carole said. "This isn't easy on any of us. Don't make it harder!"

"I know. I'm sorry. I was part of the problem. I can help be part of the solution. Lisa's right, of course. We made a solemn promise. We broke it. We have to take the consequences. So who's going to do it? Maybe we should go alphabetically by first name?"

"Or *last* name?" Carole said.

"Give me a break," said Lisa. "We do it the democratic way."

"Vote?"

"No, draw straws. Short straw invites Veronica into The Saddle Club."

She drew her feet out of the creek and then climbed down from the rock. Just to the left by the bank of the creek there was a small reedy area. Using her pocket knife, Lisa cut three lengths of the narrow reeds. Two were long—about three inches. One was short—about two inches. She mixed them up and held them in her fist, all even at the top.

"Okay, you girls pick. I'll take what's left."

Carole drew first and sighed with relief to find herself holding three inches of reed. Stevie went next. She wasn't so sure, but she held hers up to Carole's. They were the same length.

"Oh, no!" Lisa groaned, opening her fist. There lay one short piece of straw. "How about two out of three?"

"No way!" said Carole and Stevie in a single voice.

"Besides, you're the nicest one of us," Carole said. "You'll be able to make it sound as if we might actually mean it!"

"Okay, then, here's the deal," Lisa said. "I don't want to talk about it anymore right now. For the rest of our ride, we're just going to enjoy ourselves and The Saddle Club as much as we possibly can. After all, it's never going to be the same again. When we get back to Pine

Hollow and our horses are untacked and groomed and everything, you two go on over to TD's." TD's was the ice cream shop where they often had Saddle Club meetings. "I'll talk to Veronica and then bring her over there for her first official meeting. Okay?"

"Deal," Stevie said. She especially liked the part about not thinking about Veronica until after their ride was over. The longer she could put that off, the better.

3

"Coffee ice cream, butterscotch sauce, pineapple chunks, almond clusters, coconut, and marshmallow fluff."

"Maraschino cherry?"

"Of course."

Carole gulped. One of the things she hadn't missed while she was away was Stevie's sundaes. The waitress turned to her.

"Hot fudge on vanilla. Two scoops."

"Maraschino cherry?"

"No thanks." She'd keep it simple.

"Do you see them yet?" Stevie asked. Carole was facing the door and would be the first to know when Lisa was arriving with Veronica.

"She's wanted to be in our club from the very beginning," Carole said.

"It's not that she likes us, either. It's just that she can't stand the idea of being excluded from anything."

"It's going to be awful, isn't it?"

"It's never going to be the same, that's for sure," said Stevie.

"I don't think I'm really hungry."

"Veronica's always had a way of killing my appetite, too," Stevie said.

They stared glumly at one another, fiddling with their silverware, sipping their water. There wasn't much to say. They both knew how awful the situation was. The Saddle Club was very special to them because it was about horses and it was about friends. Friends were people you liked. That simply didn't include Veronica.

"Maybe we'll get to like her better when we get to know her better," Carole suggested.

"Stop trying to look on the bright side of things. We've all known her a long time and we know her well enough to know that we don't like her."

"Yeah," said Carole. She took another sip of water.

The door to TD's opened then. Veronica came in first. Lisa was right behind her. Carole waved weakly. Stevie turned around and tried to smile, but there was no welcoming warmth in her heart.

Stevie and Carole each moved over in the booth so Veronica and Lisa could sit down. Lisa sat down. Veronica remained standing.

"I just had to come over here and see you three together," Veronica said.

"Have a seat," Carole said. "And we can start the meeting."

"You can start your silly meeting when I leave," said Veronica.

Stevie wasn't sure she'd heard right, but if she had she wanted to hear more.

"You're not staying?"

"It's more like I'm not joining your dumb club," Veronica retorted. "What kind of a girl do you think I am?"

None of them thought it would be a good idea to take the bait on that question. They left it unanswered.

"I am a horsewoman!" Veronica declared with a haughtiness that was extreme even for her. "I ride whenever I can, wherever I go. I mean, last month when I was in Paris, I even rode in the Bois de Boulogne. Whatever would make you think I'd be the least bit interested in joining a group that would pledge *not* to ride for a whole month?"

There was a stunned silence. Veronica wasn't finished, though.

"So, you can have your little club all to yourselves. I suppose you thought people would begin to consider it a better group if you had me as a member. Well, I'm sorry to disappoint you, but I want no part of it at all."

With that Veronica spun on her heel and marched toward the door.

For a moment the three girls just sat there, as shocked as if a bomb had obliterated the entire town of Willow Creek. Then Stevie began to laugh, a deep belly laugh that was instantly contagious. Carole and Lisa joined in, and soon everyone in the ice cream shop was looking at them.

Just then the waitress brought Stevie and Carole's orders. She put the dishes down and asked Lisa what she'd have.

"Uh—" Lisa gasped for breath. "Hot fudge on mint chip with whipped cream," she managed to get out.

"Maraschino cherry?"

"Yes, please."

Suddenly Carole pushed her sundae across the table, back toward the waitress. She wiped the tears from her eyes, and then said politely, "Could I have a maraschino cherry, too? And maybe some whipped cream? And sprinkles?"

"Uh, sure," the waitress said, picking up Carole's sundae. She grimaced at Stevie's concoction. "Yours okay? You couldn't possibly want to add anything to that mess."

Stevie hesitated for just a second, then leaned over to place her sundae on the tray alongside her friends'. "Actually, I'd like to change mine, too. How about one more scoop and some chocolate crunchies?"

The waitress rolled her eyes before whisking away the sundaes.

Stevie's eyes were twinkling when she looked back at

her friends. "We've got a lot of catching up to do," she said with a shrug. "I might get hungry."

"Besides," Carole chimed in, "this calls for a celebration." She beamed at her two best friends and they smiled back at her.

After a long summer, mostly without horses, The Saddle Club was back in the saddle!

ABOUT THE AUTHOR

BONNIE BRYANT is the author of many books for young readers, including novelizations of movie hits such as *Teenage Mutant Ninja Turtles* and *Honey, I Blew Up the Kid*, written under her married name, B. B. Hiller.

Ms. Bryant began writing The Saddle Club in 1986. Although she had done some riding before that, she intensified her studies then and found herself learning right along with her characters Stevie, Carole, and Lisa. She claims that they are all much better riders than she is.

Ms. Bryant was born and raised in New York City. She still lives there, in Greenwich Village, with her two sons.

THE SECRET OF THE STALLION
Saddle Club Super Edition #2

It's going to be one of the most amazing adventures The Saddle Club has ever had! Stevie, Lisa, and Carole are going to horsey old England. They'll even ride in a show on the grounds of a real castle. Lisa has done some homework and discovered an ancient unsolved mystery about the duke who once lived there. The duke buried treasure under the stall of his spirited stallion. Then tragedy struck—the barn burned down and the stallion perished. A year later, the duke's body was found on the same spot, his hand clutching a single fire opal. . . . Legend says the treasure will be found by a rider with fire in his heart.

The girls are busy with the show, sightseeing in London, and getting ready for a costume ball at the castle. On that special night, it seems that almost anything could happen—but the story of the duke, his stallion, and the tragedy of the burning barn couldn't replay itself, *could it*?

Join The Saddle Club as they try to uncover the secret of the stallion.

WESTERN STAR
Saddle Club Super Edition #3

The girls of The Saddle Club can't wait for winter break from school. Carole, Stevie, and Lisa are heading west to spend the first part of their vacation at one of their favorite places—the Bar None Ranch.

But what they thought would be a quick trip turns into a snowbound adventure. The girls must rescue a herd of horses that face a terrible fate. . . .

Join The Saddle Club on an unforgettable journey that recalls the true spirit of giving and the strength of friendship.